More praise for *The Horned Man*

"For 25 years I have deliberately resisted every impulse to use the adjective 'unputdownable.' But records are meant to be broken, and James Lasdun's dark psychological thriller *The Horned Man* is . . . 'unputdownable.' . . . It is a masterpiece of chilling, mesmerizing control."   —Michael Dirda, *Washington Post*

"This is poet Lasdun's first work of fiction, but in it he displays none of the faltering or swaggering of many a debut novelist. Instead, there's a poet's willed attention to language in all its aspects: its fluency, its sound, its doubled and inverted meanings, its power simultaneously to reveal and suppress. . . . This enormously inventive, superbly written novel puts more seasoned authors in the shade."   —*The Sunday Times* (London)

"*The Horned Man* is an intelligent, original and imaginative mystery story."   —*The Economist*

"[Lasdun] employs a deft and economical pen to make this first novel succeed. It is witty, inventive, and engaging from start to finish."   —*Boston Globe*

"An exquisitely imagined thriller of the darkest hue . . . [a] brilliant portrait."   —*Seattle Times/Post Intelligencer*

"The story has all the elements of one of Hitchcock's great films . . . superb."   —*Time Out New York*

"[A] brilliantly mysterious debut novel."   —*Publishers Weekly*

"[*The Horned Man*] is like Kafka entering the *Twilight* ˌ
of literary allusions and a suspenseful plot that twists iɪ.
events and into Miller's psyche, where memory and ɪ
become ensnarled."   —*Library Journal*, starred rev

"It is necessary to read novels like this one, even when you're certain you've inhaled every possible literary maneuver. . . . With all the novel's rich details and exquisite though unaffected writing, Lasdun has brought about a work that is driven by tone, a reflection of his poetic adeptness."   —*Ruminator Review*

"A remarkable, unsettling novel."   —*Toronto Globe and Mail*

"Spectacularly unnerving, *The Horned Man* effortlessly reveals the fantastic in the quotidian, and I put this book down trusting myself less than I did before I read it."   —*New York Sun*

"A brilliant novel that must be reread at least once."
—*The Independent on Sunday*

"An exquisite and frightening book . . . *The Horned Man* is a page-turner. Not because it satisfies that comfortable cliche—a clever literary work riding on the back of a conventional thriller—but because it is driven by the compulsions of pure literature. Every page tempts you with the possibility of fulfillment, that the story will be fully explained, and so—therefore—will the world."
—*Evening Standard* (London)

"This psycho-thriller is clever, stunning and uncomfortable. Its twists had me thinking strange thoughts for days."
—*Daily Mail*

"In *The Horned Man* Lasdun has hauled out something deeply disturbing and compelling from a pristine darkness of his own."

—*The Observer*

"Lasdun's modern morality tale leaves one wanting more from this imaginative and artful writer."

—*Times Literary Supplement*

"This is a study of madness that remains disconcertingly sane. . . . Lasdun brings the same tightly woven complexity, the same veneer of restraint, to this novel as he brings to his poetry. His prose is crisp, clear, meticulously calibrated. His attention to detail is immaculate."

—*The Times* (London)

"The immediacy with which Lasdun delivers you into the heart of Miller's perplexing interior landscape reflects his mastery of the written word. The lean, staccato precision of his prose has the confidence of an experienced storyteller . . . simply travelling with this elegant weaver of words will be a pleasure."

—*The Daily Telegraph*

"A Jamesian exercise in sensibility, certainly, but with a glistening thrillerish edge. . . . [*The Horned Man*] achieves an effect comparatively rare in contemporary fiction: the feeling of someone not only thinking on the page, but communicating that thought beyond it."

—*The Guardian*

"A tale of Borgesian complexity . . . there is a pleasing interconnectedness to the plot that will delight jigsaw fanatics as they watch the story fit together with satisfying clicks."

—*The Independent*

"The Horned Man is a marvelous novel, both compellingly readable—I literally could not put it down—and deeply philosophical."

—*The Scotsman*

Also by James Lasdun

Fiction

Besieged: Selected Stories
Delirium Eclipse
Three Evenings and Other Stories

Poetry

Landscape with Chainsaw
A Jump Start
Woman Police Officer in Elevator
After Ovid: New Metamorphoses
(coedited with Michael Hofmann)

THE
HORNED
MAN

James Lasdun

W. W. Norton & Company New York London

Copyright © 2002 by James Lasdun

First published as a Norton paperback 2003

For information about permission to reproduce selections from this book,
write to Permissions, W. W. Norton & Company, Inc., 500 Fifth Avenue,
New York, NY 10110

Manufacturing by Quebecor Fairfield

Book design by Chris Welch

Production manager: Julia Druskin

Library of Congress Cataloging-in-Publication Data

Lasdun, James.

The horned man / James Lasdun. — 1st American ed.

p. cm.

1. British—New York (State)—New York—Fiction. 2. College teachers—
Fiction. 3. New York (N.Y.)—Fiction. 4. Serial murders—Fiction. I. Title.

PR6062.A735 H67 2002

823'.914—dc21   2002000539

ISBN 978-0-393-32438-9

W. W. Norton & Company, Inc., 500 Fifth Avenue, New York, N.Y. 10110

www.wwnorton.com

W. W. Norton & Company Ltd., Castle House, 75/76 Wells Street, London
W1T 3QT

3 4 5 6 7 8 9 0

THE
HORNED
MAN

Chapter 1

One afternoon earlier this winter, in a moment of idle curiosity, I took a book from the shelf in my office and began reading it where it fell open on a piece of compressed tissue that had evidently been used as a bookmark. I'd only had time to read a few sentences when I was interrupted by a knock on the door. Reluctantly—the sentences had looked interesting—I closed the book on its marker and returned it to the shelf.

The next morning I took it down again, intending to continue reading where I had left off, only to find that the marker was no longer at the page it had been on the day before. Leafing through the book, I found my sentences thirty pages earlier. Either I had moved the marker inadvertently myself, or else some night visitor had been reading the book in my absence. I settled on the first as the more likely explanation, though it seemed odd that I could have moved a bookmark thirty pages forward without noticing it.

I mentioned it that afternoon to Dr. Schrever as I lay on the crimson couch of her small consulting room off Central Park

West. After telling her the story, which she received in her cus-
tomary silence, I asked her if it might have been a case of *parapraxis*—Freud's term for the lapses of memory, slips of the
tongue, and other minor suppressions of consciousness that
occur in everyday life.

"Maybe I moved it myself, without being aware of it."

"Is that what you think happened?" Dr. Schrever asked.

"I don't know. I suppose if it is, the next question is, why
would I have done it?"

Dr. Schrever said nothing.

"You think I deliberately hid the words from myself because
they disturbed me in some way?"

"Is that what you think?"

"I suppose it's possible. . . ."

We continued like this for a little while, but the topic didn't
seem to be leading anywhere, and we moved on to other, unrelated matters.

And by the time I next went into my office, the mystery of the
moving bookmark had ceased to interest me.

A few days later I received my office phone bill through the internal mail. Glancing over the list of calls, almost all of which were
to my own number in New York, I happened to notice an unfa-
miliar area code. I was wondering who I could have been calling
at that number when I saw that the call had been made at two in
the morning; not an hour at which I had ever been in the office.

I was a little perturbed by the idea of a stranger having access
to my office and coming there in the middle of the night to make
phone calls. I didn't have anything to hide, but the intrusion
made the bland carpeted space with its metal desks and cabinets

feel momentarily strange, as though it were concealing something from me.

Until then, it hadn't crossed my mind to wonder whose books
these were on the shelves, whose files were stored in the cabinet,
even whose computer it was that sat shrouded in plastic on the
surface of the cumbrous desks arranged on one side of the room.
There were always the same things lying around these offices
when you were assigned them—books, files, letters, invitations
to talks, dog-eared old *New Yorker* cartoons, often a pair of gloves,
an umbrella . . . the residue of former occupants, leached by time
and dust of anything suggestive of a living human being.

But as I looked at the phone bill on my desk, it crossed my
mind that my visitor, who must have had a key to the room (I
always locked it when I left), might have been one of these former occupants.

On the other hand, perhaps I really *was* sharing the room:
legitimately and officially; with a colleague who worked on different days from me. Perhaps it was simply that nobody had
thought to inform me of this arrangement.

On my way to lunch I asked Amber, the intern, as casually as
I could, whether anyone besides me was using Room 106.

"No."

She looked at me as if expecting an explanation of the question. Ignoring this, I asked if she knew who had had my office
before I moved in there.

"Yes. That was Barbara."

"Barbara?"

"Barbara Hellermann. Why?"

"I—I think she may have left some things behind." I was reluctant to get into a conversation about the bookmark and the
phone number.

Amber gave me a strange look.

"Well—maybe. I mean . . . you know about her, right?"

"No?"

"She's dead."

"Oh!"

I was about to ask more when I felt the warning signs of an ailment that had been afflicting me since I had begun this job in the fall: an unpredictable and embarrassing tendency to blush. Like insomnia, the affliction had become a self-perpetuating problem. The fear of blushing had me in a state of permanent blush-readiness in which the slightest errancy of thought, conscious or unconscious, could open the blood-gates. A moment before it started, I would experience a faint lurch inside me, and with a helpless lucidity I would know that a burning crimson tide was about to start rising from my neck over my chin and cheeks, all the way up to my forehead. I would have grown a beard by now if the hair on my face were not so fair and scant.

I thanked Amber curtly and hurried away. Outside her force field, the blush command withdrew itself, and I continued pallidly down the corridor that led out of our building.

It was snowing as I walked up Central Park West from the subway station. The large flakes were few enough in number that I was aware of each individually as it drifted by, though the sky had a lurid, bruise-colored tone, as if it were getting ready to unleash something more serious.

Lights came on in windows as I passed the Dakota Building and reached the area I had once heard described as the Therapy District. Already the snow was thickening. The trees on Dr. Schrever's street had started to catch puffy snowflakes on the tips of their purple twigs—a ghostly blossom, almost luminous in the darkening air. Through the proliferating whiteness I saw a figure moving toward me: a woman, in a thick jacket, powder-blue scarf, and black skirt—leather, from the way it gleamed.

As she approached, I found myself absentmindedly eyeing her figure, a crude reflex I had been struggling to correct but still sometimes caught myself succumbing to. Her legs were slim and shapely; her hips moved in their gleaming sheath with a sinuous, swaying motion. As she drew close, I peered through the veils of snow to check out her face and saw, to my astonishment, that it was Dr. Schrever.

I was early for my appointment, so I suppose there was no reason for her not to be out on the street. But the sight of her there (I had never seen her outside the context of the consulting room) was disconcerting. She smiled at me; we said hello, and continued on our separate ways. At the end of the street I looked back and saw that she had crossed the avenue and was heading into Central Park.

I had half an hour to kill, so I stopped for a coffee at a diner on Amsterdam Avenue. As I sat in my booth I found myself thinking about the encounter. Had Dr. Schrever noticed me eyeing her up? I wondered. The thought that she might have, troubled me. She had asked me more than once whether I ever experienced sexual feelings for her, and I had told her emphatically that I hadn't. As a matter of fact, although I had spent the first few sessions sitting on a chair opposite her (rather than the couch I now lay on), I had never formed a very definite sense of her physical reality at all. She had shortish dark hair, dark eyes, smooth skin. Beyond that, her appearance always melted into vagueness whenever I tried to summon it. Agewise, for all I knew, she might have been a seasoned thirty or a well-preserved fifty. I never noticed her clothes, though I suppose I wouldn't have suspected a taste for leather skirts.

It became clear to me now that in her capacity as my therapist, I had placed her off-limits sexually, but that reduced to the anonymity of a female human being, she was in fact quite capable of arousing desire in me after all.

These two aspects had been separated as I watched her coming toward me through the snow. I pictured her again, trying to catch the carefree, sensual elegance she had projected before I realized who she was. A distinct pang of arousal went through me. And at once a preposterous surmise came into my head: she changed into the leather skirt between sessions to pick up men and have sex with them for money in the park. I could go there now and find her with one knee provocatively cocked as she leaned pale and delicately shivering against a cedar post of the trellised walkway that led down to the lake. . . .

I finished my coffee, read a newspaper, then walked the two blocks to her building. As I entered her consulting room, I saw that she had changed her clothes again: in place of the leather skirt was a demure pleated tweed affair, with thick brown wool tights underneath and house slippers on her feet. She looked rather aloof and forbidding.

I lay down on the couch, facing away from her. For a moment I almost balked at telling her the things that had just been going through my mind, but at a hundred dollars an hour, I couldn't afford to suppress anything that might prove illuminating.

"After I passed you on the street just now," I began, "I went to a diner where I started thinking about why seeing you like that disturbed me, which it did, and I found myself drifting into this fantasy. . . ."

I described all the things I had thought and felt and imagined as I sat in the diner. As I spoke, I was aware of the sound of her pen scratching across the pages of the notebook she always jot-

ted in furiously while I talked. It occurred to me that this notebook contained a great deal of intimate material about me, and
I wondered if there were any circumstances under which she
would show it to someone else. Was she bound by any code of
privacy or therapist's version of the Hippocratic oath? What, in
fact, bound her to me other than the fees I paid her; the fees I
realized now I had been faintly annoyed to see glistening in that
expensive-looking leather skirt?

I must have been speaking for longer than I realized: it seemed
we had barely begun to discuss my fantasy of her picking up men
in the park when a soft buzzing filled the room, marking the
arrival of Dr. Schrever's next patient.

As I got up to go, Dr. Schrever looked at me in a way that
seemed for a moment uneasy.

"By the way," she said, "I wasn't sure whether to tell you this,
but I think on balance I should. You mentioned passing me in the
street, but I haven't been out of this room all afternoon."

I looked at her, dumbstruck.

"In any case," she went on, "I was with another patient when
you arrived. You must have seen him leave while you were in the
waiting room."

Now that I thought of it, I had seen him leave: a lugubrious-
looking man who always preceded me that day of the week. But
so certain had I been of encountering Dr. Schrever half an hour
earlier that it hadn't even crossed my mind to infer from his presence anything that might have brought this into question. I had
seen him, but apparently not taken account of him.

"Perhaps it disturbs you to think I have other customers?" she
asked, looking at me levelly.

"You mean . . . patients?"

"Well, yes," she said with the trace of a smile, and I realized she had been referring lightheartedly to my fantasy, presumably to defuse any embarrassment I might have felt about it, with a note of humor, and I appreciated this.

Even so, as I left, I felt rather worried that I could have made such a blatant error of recognition, and as I walked back toward the park, where the snow was now lying in raised veins along every shiny black branch and twig, forming an exact white replica of each tree, I wondered who the woman was who had smiled at me in the street and said hello.

I walked idly over to the opening where I had seen her disappear into the park, and even went so far as to go down the winding path that led to the lake.

There was a small, rustic shelter where the path turned. I looked in; half-hoping, I suppose, to see the woman there. It was empty, of course. I stood there for a moment, watching the snowflakes dissolving in the black water, parts of which still had great plates of ice floating on or just under the surface.

Then I went home.

The next time I was in my office, I made a deliberate effort to settle the question of whether there really were grounds for thinking I had an intruder. The moving bookmark no longer seemed very mysterious, and given my misidentification of Dr. Schrever I now began to wonder whether I might not have been paying proper attention when I went through the phone bill. Perhaps I had called that number after all, forgotten whose it was, and misread the time of night recorded on the printout. I looked for the bill now, but I couldn't find it. I assumed I must have thrown it away after paying it, and the cleaner had emptied the wastepaper basket.

In the act of searching for it, however, I found myself for the first time really noticing the contents of this room. It hadn't occurred to me to take stock of them before; after all, why would anyone waste a moment on such things—objects so remote from any active use or ownership, they'd staled away into little more than dust-shrouded memories of themselves? But my curiosity was aroused, and I embarked on a conscious inventory of the place.

Black-stained wooden chairs and bookcases; off-white walls; gray carpet and doors; a four-drawer metal filing cabinet with a Hewlett-Packard printer curled up on top of it; the two oversized desks by the latticed window, a Dell desktop computer on one of them, on the other a giant stapler; a five- to seven-cup Hot Pot coffeemaker in its opened box; my own wooden desk with cables running around its legs and a cache of Styrofoam peanuts under its base—out of reach of the cleaner's vacuum.

There was a door I hadn't opened: behind it a closet with an air conditioner hibernating on the floor, pleated wings folded neatly into its body. Some clothes in a dry cleaner's wrap hung on a metal hanger from a peg, under a woman's maroon beret. The late Barbara Hellermann's, perhaps? I closed that door. A few curled and fading cards stood on the window ledge. I opened them; saw they were all to Barbara from her students: *Thank you for being you; Your generosity and understanding will live with me forever.* A clock in the shape of a sunflower stood on a metal shelf next to several amateurish, brightly glazed pottery mugs. Although these things were of little interest in themselves, I did find it interesting that I hadn't even registered them until now. On another shelf was a bronze bowl with pebbles, a piece of quartz, a fir cone, a tarnished coin—Bulgarian, on closer inspection— a key ring, and a jay feather. There was a framed Matisse still-life on the wall, a small cork bulletin board with an old teaching schedule pinned to it, and next to that a rough-edged

square of what looked like hand-made paper with the following
quotation printed on it in gold letters:

> I want to do something splendid. Something heroic or
> wonderful, that won't be forgotten after I'm dead.
> I think I shall write books.
> —*Louisa May Alcott*

The ceiling was made of perforated white drop tiles and was
stained yellow from a leak in one corner. The light came from
three plastic-paneled fluorescent strips.

Completing my examination of the room without any great
sense of satisfied curiosity, I found myself thinking of Barbara
Hellermann. I pictured her coming in here, hanging up her beret
and her dry cleaning, glancing cheerfully at her cards, her uplifting quotation, taking her five- to seven-cup Hot Pot from its box
to brew coffee in for her class, setting out the pottery mugs. . . .
The sense of a sweet-natured, diligent soul came into me. I imagined her as an elderly lady, and hoped that her death had been
peaceful.

Chapter 2

Later that week I attended a meeting of the Sexual Harassment Committee. It was unusual for someone as new to the job as I was to serve on this committee, but I had sat on the Disciplinary Committee at a previous job in Louisiana, and it was thought that my experience there might be useful here, so that when a seat had fallen vacant at the beginning of this semester, I had been invited to take it.

I had hesitated before accepting. I had had a taste of the hostility one is liable to receive in return for doing this kind of work. In Louisiana, at a clambake on college grounds, a senior professor had overheard a sophomore warning some freshmen about the chiggers—insects that burrow under your skin; a local hazard. Without stopping to think, the professor had blurted out a foolish witticism: "We're not allowed to call them chiggers anymore," he had said, guffawing. "We have to call them chegroes."

It hadn't taken the students long to find their way past the smirk of glib humor in this to the leer of racism lurking beneath it, and before the party was over they had lodged a protest with the student council. The matter was brought before the Disciplinary Committee, and we agreed unanimously that the joke was a speech act showing an implicit contempt for the sensitivities of minority students. The professor was asked to make a written apology, but instead of doing so he had resigned—a gesture that aroused a storm of publicity in the local press. For several weeks the members of the Disciplinary Committee, myself included, had been pilloried as fanatics of the new religion of Political Correctness. Given the low level of reporting in these newspapers, not to mention the extreme reactionary position they took on all social issues, this wasn't as painful as it might sound—there was even a certain sense of martyred righteousness to be had from it—but I hadn't much enjoyed the experience, and the thought of exposing myself to a possible repetition of it up here at Arthur Clay College didn't greatly appeal.

What decided me in the end was the sense that as a teacher of gender studies, instructing my students in the science of unscrambling the genetic code of prejudice, false objectivity, and pernicious sexual stereotyping that forms the building blocks of so many of our cultural monuments, I had an ethical obligation to follow through on my intellectual principles into the realm of real human relations, where these hidden codes wrought their true, devastating effects—or at any rate not to refuse to do so when asked. Either I believed that what I did for a living had a basis in life itself, or else I was wasting my time.

I knew, of course, that the proceedings of these committees had by now become a stock-in-trade object of satire in popular plays and novels, but once I had made up my mind to serve, I found that I cared only as much about this as I had about the Louisiana newspapers: not enough to balk at doing what I considered my duty. It was a matter, finally, of standing up and being counted.

Sexual Harassment Awareness Week was in two months' time, and the first part of our meeting was taken up with our two student representatives outlining proposals for Take Back the Night events, date rape seminars, a speech code conference, and so on.

After we had voted to support and finance these proposals, the students left us and we proceeded to discuss what our chair, Roger Freeman, described as a "delicate matter." This turned out to concern a young lecturer who was said to be engaging in sexual relations with several of his students. As yet there had been no formal complaints, but the rumors in circulation suggested it was only a matter of time.

The lecturer, a fellow Englishman named Bruno Jackson, was aware of the rules governing this sort of conduct. He and I had both attended the sexual harassment seminar, obligatory for all new faculty, at the beginning of the year. There, we were addressed by Elaine Jordan, the school attorney (and a member of this committee), on the need for constant vigilance and self-scrutiny. She advised us to keep our office doors wide open during one-on-one meetings with students of either sex. She urged us to look around our desks for objects of an inadvertently suggestive nature that might offend or upset a sensitive student. As an example, she gave the case of a visiting Australian adjunct who had written the word "Ramses," the name of a condom brand, on the chalkboard behind him. Two or three of his students had been made uncomfortable by this, imagining it to be some kind of Australian method of importuning. When the man was brought before the Sexual Harassment Committee, he expressed astonishment, claiming the word referred to a Turkish cigarette of the same name, which a friend had asked him to buy in New York, and that he had chalked it up to remind himself. To the extent that he wasn't officially reprimanded, he had been given the benefit of the doubt, but his contract had not been renewed. "And be advised," Elaine had continued, "these things stay in your record. Permanently."

She had then gone on to warn us about the dangers of introducing the subject of sex into classroom discussions. "Obviously you can't always avoid it, but be sensitive. Some students find it embarrassing, especially when they think a faculty member's harping on the subject unnecessarily. We get a lot of complaints about teachers who are always looking for the sexual symbolism of a poem or story—"

It was here that Bruno Jackson had interrupted her. I had already noticed him reacting with ill-concealed amazement and sarcastic disbelief to much of what Elaine had been telling us, as though it were the first time he had encountered anything like this, which was unlikely, given the peripatetic job history he and I shared. I myself had heard numerous versions since coming to the States from England seven years ago, and was no more surprised by it than I would have been, say, by a flight attendant demonstrating safety procedures before takeoff.

"Wait a minute," he'd said in a voice brimming with aggressive irony. "Are you saying I have to put a lid on discussion of sexual imagery in the books I teach?"

Elaine looked at him, startled. She saw herself as our ally—a purveyor of information necessary to our survival—and it clearly upset her to be spoken to as an oppressor.

"No, that isn't what I'm saying." Her eyes darted anxiously about the room in search of support. "I'm just saying you have to be sensitive."

I nodded vigorously, and one or two other people followed suit.

"The kids don't like being made to feel uncomfortable," Elaine continued. "They're very young, remember. Not even in their twenties, some of them—"

"I see," Bruno had said. "So, for instance, I'm teaching Jane Austen this week. *Mansfield Park*. There's this one scene where a girl loses something down the back of a sofa. She pushes her hand down the cracks between the cushions and starts feeling around for it. It's all very heightened, and as far as I'm concerned it's a thinly veiled image of female masturbation. Are you saying I should just gloss over that?"

Elaine, who had recovered her composure now, gave him a level stare. "All I'm trying to do," she said, "is I'm trying to alert you to the possible consequences of certain acts. I'm not here to tell you how to teach your classes. That's a judgment call only you can make."

"I'll take that as a veto on masturbation in Jane Austen, then," Bruno had said with a smirk. He'd looked around the room, as though expecting complicit smiles. I avoided his eye, and as far as I could tell, not one of us, male or female, had given him the slightest hint of encouragement.

After the meeting I had gone up to compliment Elaine on her handling of the situation. She thanked me profusely. We talked for a while—about what, I forget, though I do remember thinking that she was a more vulnerable and emotional person than her somewhat bland exterior had suggested.

Looking back at Bruno's behavior, I see that it wouldn't have been difficult to predict the trouble that was now looming over him.

Roger Freeman, our chair, was a small, dapper man of about fifty, with sparkling blue eyes and a thick mane of white hair. He had a dry, fluent way of talking, as though his words had formed themselves long before he actually spoke them, and he was merely reporting his side of a conversation that had already taken place.

"Here's what I think we need to do," he began. "Number one,

we need to talk informally to this young man, give him a chance to explain what's going on here. Number two . . . "

It was my job, as the newest member of the committee, to keep the minutes at these meetings. I was an assiduous clerk, and in my efforts to write down everything that was said, I often didn't take any of it in until after the meeting was over. I didn't, for instance, register the name "Trumilcik," a name that was to become increasingly important to me over the next weeks, until later, when I was checking the legibility of my minutes prior to giving them to the department secretary to type out.

What we need to avoid at all costs, I saw that Roger had said, *is letting things get to the point where we find ourselves with another Trumilcik on our hands.*

"Who's Trumilcik?" I asked Marsha, the department secretary.

"Bogomil Trumilcik? Oh, God! What do you want to know about him for?"

I smiled. "You'll see when you read this." I handed her the minutes.

Marsha was a large woman with a resonant voice.

"He was a visiting professor. Some kind of poet or novelist from Romania or Bulgaria or one of those places. He was an awful man. I mean just awful!"

"What did he do?" This was Amber, looking up from her desk at the side of the room. Remembering my near-blush of the other day, I refrained from looking at her. But I was strongly conscious of her presence—her sleepy eyes, her short reddish-orange hair dividing in soft feathery wisps down the fluted back of her neck, her skin freckled and unnaturally pale, almost silvery. Acknowledging to myself that this young woman had begun to have an effect on me, and preferring to confront such things rather than sweep them under the rug, I made a mental note to think about the precise nature of this effect, and to construct a suitable attitude in response.

"What *didn't* he do!" Marsha was saying. "He made passes at practically every female he taught. Then when someone finally complained about him to the president, instead of being embarrassed, he went totally crazy. He made this terrible commotion right out there on campus. I mean the most truly awful scene you can imagine. Him yelling at the president, calling everyone the most horrible names, students yelling at him . . . just awful! Finally he ran off down Mulberry Street, screaming and yelling like a madman."

"What happened to him?" I asked.

"He never showed up again. They had to find another instructor to take over his classes."

It wasn't until I got back to my office that the real significance of Marsha's story struck me. I was sitting down at my desk when the bronze bowl on one of the black-stained shelves caught my eye and I remembered the Bulgarian coin I had seen in it.

I went over to the bowl to look again at the coin. The pebbles were there as I had left them, as were the quartz, the fir cone, the key ring, and the jay feather. But the coin was gone.

Given my recent spate of slips and lapses, my first inclination was to think I must have made another mistake. Either there'd been no coin in the first place, and I had somehow fabricated a memory of it, or else there had been a coin, but for some reason I myself had spirited it away, behind my own back.

The first seemed inconceivable: I could remember with absolute clarity the physical appearance of the coin—the high-domed head of some dignitary on one side, the bunch of grapes on the other, the Cyrillic letters I had partially deciphered using the smattering of ancient Greek I still remembered from school. Also the feel of it in my hand—the almost total weightlessness of the silver-gray alloy it was cast in; more like plastic than metal. How could I have invented such a vivid and detailed memory? It simply wasn't possible. As to the latter, that I myself had got rid of the coin, although it seemed far-fetched, I had to admit that on the basis of my having moved the bookmark and misread the phone number—if those were indeed what had occurred in these cases—not to mention misidentified Dr. Schrever on the street, which indubitably *had* occurred, this too was possible. But what reason could I have had for doing it—especially since I'd have had to have done it *before* I'd heard of Trumilcik, or at any rate learned that he may have been Bulgarian? I had no prior connection to Bulgaria, and I could think of no other earthly reason why I should want to conceal a coin from myself. It didn't make sense.

And yet I still couldn't give myself entirely to the belief that someone else had been in the room and taken it.

Mystified, I set off for the train station, a ten-minute walk.

Last week's snow had mostly melted, leaving just a few rags of soot-flecked white in the shadows of walls and hedges. The campus was landscaped to give the impression of a pastoral setting, though it was in the middle of a dreary town that was itself part of the uninterrupted sprawl running west and north from New York. It had been founded by a local sugar merchant at the turn of the last century, as a memorial to a beloved nephew, Arthur Clay, who had died young, and after whom the college was named. Something of the fluky nature of its origins (if the boy hadn't died, the college presumably wouldn't be there) still clung to it despite its massive shade trees and thick-walled gothic buildings. In winter especially, with the traffic and nearby housing projects unhidden by foliage, you felt the thinness of the romantic illusion of itself—something between a country estate

and a medieval seat of learning—that it seemed intent on pur-
veying; its closeness to nonexistence.

In the parking lot I saw Amber, heading out onto Mulberry
Street. She was drifting along at her usual sleepwalker's pace. I
hadn't had a chance to think about her effect on me yet, and by
default fell into the perhaps regrettable but, alas, necessary attitude of caution a man in my position needs to adopt in such sit-
uations. I felt that it would be unwise to be seen walking with her
off the campus, but on the other hand I didn't wish to seem
unfriendly by passing her by, so I slowed down to a dawdle, letting her get a couple of hundred yards ahead of me. As a result I
missed my train and had half an hour to wait till the next one.

Time to kill. I disliked having nothing to do. I walked to the
end of the platform and back; looked at my watch: a minute and
a half had passed. A familiar vague restlessness came into me.
The blank oblong of time ahead of me seemed to thicken, forming a viscous, impenetrable emptiness. I didn't want to have to
think about the things I inevitably thought about during these
dead stretches. Up above the opposite platform five cold pigeons
snuggled in a row on top of a rain-puckered billboard with a
podiatrist's ad on it: 1-800-WHY HURT? 1-800-END PAIN.

Trumilcik . . . the name stirred in my mind again. . . . I thought
of him running off down Mulberry Street, *screaming and yelling
like a madman*. Where had he run to? The train station? Had he
stood here like me, waiting for a train into Manhattan? And if so,
then what? Packed his bags and booked the next flight back to
Bulgaria?

I doubted that. I had met very few visiting workers in this
country who had the slightest interest in returning to their native
land unless they were forced to. The mind abhors a vacuum: into
the total vacuum that represented my knowledge of Bulgaria
spread the one detail I had recently encountered, namely the

coin—its submetallic substance, pallid color (as if leached of any purchasing power), the squat, handicapped-looking lettering, the blandly pompous face on one side of it, the bunch of implausibly circular grapes on the other—and it seemed to me distinctly unlikely that a man who had put all that behind him would choose to return to it if he could possibly avoid doing so.

I found myself imagining Trumilcik surreptitiously entering my office late at night. I pictured him sitting at my desk, reading the book I had taken from the shelf, using the phone. . . . I thought of him removing the coin from the bronze bowl. As I did so, something delicately uneasy passed through me, though as I tried to account for it, the sensation—too faint to withstand scrutiny—evaporated.

Six and a half minutes. . . . A high-speed train bulleted through the station, pummeling the air. The pigeons shifted in unison, ruffling their feathers a little before settling back as they were, as if they thought it only polite to register such an event.

There was a pay phone on the platform. I'd been resisting its winking glitter since I'd arrived, but I found myself starting to amble toward it. As I did, I saw myself dialing my wife's number. I heard her voice say hello, then imagined asking her in a casual tone how she was doing; telling her I just happened to be thinking of her, waiting to see if she would suggest getting together for dinner, realizing she wasn't going to, and saying a friendly, brittle goodbye, with a reinvigorated sense of the emptiness of the evening that lay ahead of me.

Better not to call, I told myself as I approached the phone. Better to think she might for once have actually suggested the dinner if only I *had* called. That way when I ate I could legitimately imagine her right there across the table.

But I continued moving toward the phone.

I was within a few feet of it, resigning myself to my own weakness in the weary way one does at the point of giving in to a vice, when a colorful, chattering group of people arrived on the platform. All but one were students, sporting an array of clownish hats and the exaggeratedly baggy clothes that had briefly gone out of style, only to return with a vengeance.

The other figure, short and stocky in a black winter coat, was none other than Bruno Jackson.

Seeing me, he smiled warmly and strolled over, his young posse following loudly behind him.

I had had little contact with him this semester, but he was always friendly when we ran into each other. I felt that he hadn't given up hope of recruiting me as an ally. The fact that we were both English seemed to mean something to him. Though he had been in the States several years longer than I had, and seemed in many ways thoroughly Americanized (his accent had warped into an ugly transatlantic hybrid that made me feel protective about the purity of my own), he retained an interest in British popular culture, which he seemed to assume I shared. I remember listening to him talk volubly about a new cable show featuring British darts tournaments, and trying politely to match his enthusiasm, while all I really felt was the familiar melancholy that most things English seemed to arouse in me ever since I'd first arrived in the States as an Abramowitz Fellow at Columbia University. Now, of course, there was a more serious difference between us. I don't know if he realized I was on the Sexual Harassment Committee, but from my point of view the fact that I was made a friendship with him out of the question.

His cheery approach right now was particularly disconcerting. Given the discussion concerning him at the meeting I'd just attended, I felt that it would compromise me to be seen fraternizing with him, especially with this entourage of students milling at close quarters all around him. I was also afraid that I would be setting myself up to look treacherous if I were friendly to him now, only to be sitting in judgment on him in a few weeks' time.

"Going into the city, Lawrence?" he asked, helping himself to a cigarette from a packet that a girl—a sophomore I recognized from one of my own classes—had just taken from her embroidered backpack.

"Yes."

"Us too."

I smiled, saying nothing.

The students seemed to grow subdued in my presence. Naturally I was curious to know what they were doing traveling to New York with their instructor—an unusual if not actually illicit occurrence. But I was worried that if I asked, it might appear subsequently as though I had been looking for incriminating information.

"Where in the city do you live?" Bruno asked me.

When I told him the East Village, his tawny green eyes lit up.

"That's where we're headed too."

"Oh." I noticed that the skirt of his long coat divided at the back in a strangely baroque fashion, with two long swallowtails of thick black wool hanging from a raised lip of rectangular material.

"We're going to a play: *Blumfeld, an Elderly Bachelor,* an adaptation of a Kafka story we're reading. Do you know it?"

"No."

"Oh, wow!" one of the students said; a short, plump girl in a Peruvian wool cap. "You have to read it!"

Another student, a boy with a hatchet face and shifty, narrow eyes, began to tell me the story:

"It's about this lonely old guy who goes home to his apartment one night to find these two balls bouncing around the place all by themselves. It's hilarious. . . ."

The train came, and I felt compelled to sit with Bruno and his students. The Peruvian-hatted girl took out a camcorder and pointed it through the scratched window. An oily, ice-graveled creek ran along the tracks, full of half-swallowed car wrecks and dumped appliances.

"Hello Tomorrow . . ." sang another girl—a blond waif.

"C'mon, man, it's beautiful!" the shifty-eyed boy said.

They turned the camera on Bruno, who blew it a kiss, then on me. I gave a polite smile.

"How's Carol?" Bruno asked. I'd forgotten his prior acquaintance with my wife—the two of them had met several years back, at the Getty Institute.

"She's fine." I wasn't about to tell him we were separated.

"Why don't you come to the play? Bring her along."

I thanked him but said we couldn't.

He grinned back at the camcorder: "Professor Miller's snubbing us."

The students laughed.

Night had fallen by the time I reached my block down between B and C. It had been a crack block when Carol and I had moved there a few years ago—vials all over the sidewalk like mutant hailstones; stocky, stud-collared dealers in the doorways with canine versions of themselves grimacing on leather-and-chain leashes; a false bodega with an unchanging display of soap powders gathering dust in the window and a steady stream of human wreckage staggering in and out through the door . . . all gone now; swept clean by a mayor who seemed (so it occurs to me

now) to have modeled himself on Angelo in *Measure for Measure*,
cleaning up the stews of Vienna. I studied that play for "O" Level
English and it has stuck in my mind like no other book has since.
*Our natures do pursue, like rats that ravin down their proper bane,
a thirsty evil, and when we drink we die*: Claudio waiting to have
his head chopped off for getting a girl pregnant. The bodega was
now a cybercafé, the shooting gallery on the corner was a wheat-
grass juicery, and the crackhouse opposite had been turned into
a health and fitness center.

As I climbed the stairs to my apartment—a sixth-floor walk-
up—I thought how unpleasant this utterly lonely life was becoming. The few friends I'd made in New York had all been scattered
by the job centrifuge that rules over American lives, or else been
driven out to the suburbs by the advent of children. A part of me
regretted not having been able to accept Bruno's invitation. It
would have been out of the question, naturally, but I couldn't
help a faint wistful pang at the thought of them all sitting hap-
pily together, watching the play.

Having nothing better to do, I decided to read the story it was
based on. Carefully avoiding looking at the answering machine
on the window ledge (as long as I didn't know for sure that Carol
hadn't called, I could legitimately tell myself that she might
have), I went to my bookshelf and took down my edition of
Kafka's short works, where I found the story.

It was a very strange story, but almost stranger than the story
itself, with its two fantastical blue-veined balls following Blumfeld around his apartment, was the fact that, contrary to what I
had told Bruno, I evidently *had* read it. And not only read it, but
taught it too, as it was all marked up in little underlinings and
scribbles in my handwriting. Even so, not one word of it seemed
familiar to me now. Nothing!

It's not quite pointless after all to live in secret as an unnoticed bachelor, I read, *now that someone, no matter who, has penetrated this secret and sent him these two strange balls....* How could I have forgotten something so strikingly bizarre? A complete mental evacuation must have taken place. I simply didn't recognize a word of it. To get rid of the balls, Blumfeld plays a trick on them—climbing backward into the wardrobe so that they have to bounce in there too: *And when Blumfeld, having by now pulled the door almost to, jumps out of it with an enormous leap such as he has not made for years, slams the door, and turns the key, the balls are imprisoned.* Relieved, wiping the sweat from his brow, Blumfeld leaves the apartment. *It is remarkable how little he worries about the balls now that he is separated from them....*

Abruptly, before I had finished the story, a small, pulsating silver spot appeared in the corner of my field of vision.

I hadn't experienced this phenomenon since I was twelve or thirteen, but I recognized it immediately, and put the book down with a feeling of alarm.

The spot began to grow, as I had feared it would, flickering and pulsating across my vision like a swarm of angry insects. I stood in the middle of my living room, looking helplessly through the window as this apparition gradually blocked out the ailanthus tree in the courtyard and the lit windows of the apartments opposite. After a while all I could see were a few peripheral slivers of the ceiling and walls surrounding me. And then for a minute or two I became completely blind.

I stood, trying to remain calm, listening to the suddenly pronounced sounds of the night—monkey-yelping police sirens, the ventilator humming on the roof of the pizza kitchen across the courtyard. Above me my upstairs neighbor, Mr. Kurwen, turned on a TV, then walked heavily across his apartment to turn on a second TV. A toilet flushed next door. Then, as rapidly as it had come, the occlusion faded. And right on cue, as the last traces vanished, my head began to throb with an ache so intense I cried aloud with pain.

I had had these migraines for a period as a boy: the same silvery swarm spreading until it blinded me, then vanishing, leaving behind a headache of excruciating ferocity that continued unabated for five or six hours. After all other medications failed, my mother had taken me to a homeopathic doctor, an old Finn in a peculiar-smelling room, surrounded by dishes of felspar and a sticky substance he told me was crushed red ants. He gave me five tiny pills, instructing me to take one a night, five nights in a row. I hadn't had a migraine since then—not until now.

I went into the bedroom and lay down on the bed in darkness. The pain concentrated itself in the center of my forehead. It felt as though something were in there trying to get out—using now a hammer, now a pickaxe, now an electric drill. Above me Mr. Kurwen's two TVs came booming down through the flimsy Sheetrock walls. This had been going on since his wife had died a few months earlier. I'd gone up there to complain once, at midnight. Mr. Kurwen had opened the door, glaring impenitently. His round, white-stubbled moon of a face had something odd about it—a glass eye, I'd realized after a moment: brighter and bluer than its brother. Several lapdogs yapped in the dark behind him, where the two TVs threw lurid bouquets of color on opposing walls. "My wife just died of cancer and you're telling me to turn down the TV?" was all he had said.

Between the cacophony up there and the pounding under my forehead, I felt as if I were being slowly compressed in a room with contracting walls. What had been in the Finn's little pills? I wondered. With the confused logic of the afflicted, I tried to think what substance might have a homeopathic relationship with this particular form of pain. Caffeine, I decided: too much coffee sometimes gave me a headache. I got up, grabbed my coat, and went out. Soft, wet grains of sleet were falling thickly, clinging like icy burrs. I'd intended to go to the Polish coffee shop two blocks away, but under the circumstances I went straight into the cybercafé instead—my first visit—and ordered a triple espresso.

The place was full of well-heeled-looking kids in neat black sweaters and slacks. Of the two or three definable new generations that had come up since my own, this one made me the most anxious. In their presence I felt for the first time the obscure sense of disgrace that comes with age. Their smooth, pin-pupiled faces were splashed blue-gray from the screens; their slim, angular limbs moving elegantly between keyboard, mouse, beverage, Palm Pilot; clicking away as if they and these appurtenances had coevolved over many millennia. Some of them wore discreet brushed-steel headsets, adding to the general entomological appearance. As I drank my coffee, watching a group of them mill out through the door like a detachment of plutocratic ants, something caught my eye. Among the mosaic of flyers pinned to a bulletin board in the corner was a poster for a play. *Blumfeld, an Elderly Bachelor,* it read, *by Franz Kafka.*

In smaller print, under the bleary image of a man inside a closet, were the words: *adapted for the stage by Bogomil Trumilcik.*

Trumilcik! Seeing the name again, I felt a faint inward shift or lurch, as of a distant gear engaging. The fleeting unease I had felt at the train station returned to me, and this time—taking it, as it were, by surprise—I saw what should have been obvious to me in the first place: that the disappearance of the coin from the bronze bowl could only mean that my recent awakening to the fact of Trumilcik had prompted a reciprocal awakening in him to the fact of me. Furthermore, I couldn't help feeling that his removal of the coin (assuming I was right in attributing that action to him) had something aggressive about it, or at least aggressively defensive, as though he either wished to threaten me or else perceived me as a threat. At any rate, this unexpected reappearance of his name before me seemed, in my inflamed state, like a summons to action of my own.

I stood up and paid. The coffee was flittering and sparking in my head, adding an effect of lightning to the dry thunder already pounding there. Outside, I headed north and east, away from the gentrified blocks, to the Alphabet City I knew of old, with its charred tenements and smoldering graffiti. Even here, though, you felt the touch of the new order prevailing in City Hall. Women used to stand on the corners where the cross streets met Avenue C: junkies with microskirts over their skeletal thighs; crack-addicted mothers from the East River projects, tottering around on high heels, eyes aglitter. Gone now, like the bawds in Vienna after Angelo's proclamation against vice. The only things glittering there these days were the freshly refurbished pay phones, tricked out in their Bell Atlantic decals, silver coils and bellies gleaming in the streetlights. I gave them a wide berth, plunging on through the thick sleet still splashing down like icy paint, till I came to the theater, a modest-looking establishment in the basement of what appeared to be a derelict synagogue.

Down the stairs, through a bruised-looking metal door, was a neon-lit lobby with an empty chair at a table bearing programs and a roll of tickets. Off this was a self-closing double door. I put my ear to it, but it had been soundproofed and I could hear only muffled, incomprehensible voices. I would have opened it, but I didn't want to risk being seen by Bruno and his friends and having to explain myself later on.

A fresh cannonade of pain burst in my head: the caffeine didn't seem to be working. As I stood there, wondering what to do, a man appeared, dressed in a shabby black suit. He was about my age, with odd, pasty skin and white hands. He lit a cigarette and looked at me with a secretive expression that I took for distrust.

"What do you want?"

"Well, I—"

"The show's half over."

I decided to come straight to the point:

"I was actually trying to find out about Bogomil Trumilcik."

The man eyed me, puffing at his cigarette.

"What did you want to know?"

"Well . . . where he is, for one thing."

"Are you a friend of his?"

I looked at him. I dislike lying and am very bad at it, and even though a white lie might have helped me at that moment, I couldn't bring myself to tell one.

"More a colleague," I said, "or ex-colleague. I teach at Arthur Clay."

"Uh-huh." Again something secretive, almost sly, in the man's expression. I had a vague feeling I might have seen him somewhere before.

"Well, he's in Bulgaria," he said with an air of finality.

"Are you sure?"

"Excuse me?"

"I mean are you sure he isn't in New York?"

"Why would he be in New York?" Evidently I had given him an excuse to take offense and stonewall me. I changed my tack.

"Can I ask how you came across his adaptation?"

"Of the story? I have no idea. You'd have to ask the director."

"Ah. I was thinking you might be the director." I said this more in an attempt to flush something—anything—out of him before I left than because I really had been thinking any such thing.

"Me? No. I'm Blumfeld."

I realized then that the pastiness on his skin was makeup. Even so, I was thrown: I'd pictured the Blumfeld of the original story as a much older man. He glanced at a clock above the entrance.

"I have to go back on in a moment." He flashed me a grin. "Just time for a quick smoke before the girls find my balls."

Mildly exasperated, my head hurting more than ever, I turned to go.

"May I take a program?"

"Please. Help yourself."

I took one of the programs.

"Are you by any chance suffering from migraine?" The man asked as I moved off.

The question stopped me in my tracks.

"How did you know?"

"Your eyelids are all puffed up and your lips are almost white. My brother had migraines as a kid. I know the symptoms. Here, if you'll allow me . . ."

To my surprise, he put his hands on my temples, pressing both thumbs into the center of my forehead, extremely hard. For a moment I thought my skull was about to split. Then suddenly, magically, the pain lifted. As it did, an unexpected wave of emotion passed through me, as though some sweet intimacy, dreamlike in its utter mysteriousness, had just occurred between us.

I thanked him, amazed. He shrugged, smiling pleasantly.

"I'll try to get word to Trumilcik that you're looking for him," he said. "Now I have to run."

"Thank you. My name's Lawrence Miller," I called after him. He gave an indistinct sound as he disappeared.

Outside, I felt light-headed, almost elated. I moved quickly. I didn't want to go home. The pain may have vanished, but the caffeine was still racing around inside me. Thinking over my conversation with Blumfeld, I realized his evasiveness on the subject of Trumilcik had done nothing to dispel my impression that the man was still in New York; if anything, it had reinforced it. I realized I had even begun to form a tentative image of Trumilcik's circumstances—one that was no doubt influenced by a certain low-grade but persistent destitution-anxiety I myself had been afflicted by since coming to New York. I pictured him hanging on defiantly to some marginal, semi-illegal existence in the city; lodged in an obscure outer neighborhood and making covert nocturnal visits to his old office at Arthur Clay, to work or read his books. The thought of him still here excited me curiously, presenting itself as the sense of a door still open. And as though lit by that opening, another doorway presented itself in my mind; one that I hadn't noticed before, or at least hadn't thought of as a doorway.

I headed over to Astor Place and took the subway to the train station. It wasn't late—nine or nine-thirty—and there were still plenty of trains out to the suburbs.

A different crowd from the suit- and skirt-clad commuters waited under the Departures board. Somber-faced, with the drained pallor that comes from hard indoor labor. Evening-shift office cleaners, I guessed, movers and lifters for the big department stores, hernia-protection braces under their puff parkas. My train was announced, and I followed a group of them down to the track. They got out at stations servicing apartment complexes of crumbling cement with the bare iron bones showing through, or row housing built right up to the rail tracks. I watched them with a familiar apprehensive curiosity, sensing through them the vertiginous edge of that abyss of desolation one is never very far from in this country.

A light snow had fallen by the time I reached Arthur Clay, freshening up the sullied mounds and slush islands I'd passed earlier.

I'd never been on campus this late. It felt surprisingly subdued, low-key—no evidence of the saturnalian revelry one assumes goes on in these places at night; just a few students scurrying here and there between the dorms.

My department building was dark except for some nightlights burning dimly in the silent corridors. I made my way down to Room 106 feeling oddly furtive, even though I had a perfect right to be there. There's something you only notice about a building when it's empty except for you—the singularities of its stillness and silence; the particular qualities its walls have absorbed from the lives unfolding inside it. What I sensed here was a frosty aloofness bordering on hostility, as though it took a dim view of my presence inside it at this untimely hour.

I opened the door to my room and turned on the light. The place seemed to blink, startled almost, as if disturbed in some furtive activity of its own.

But there it all was, after all, just as I had left it a few hours earlier—the cabinets and shelves, the unremarkable bric-a-brac. And there, on one of the two large desks over by the window, deceptively bland-looking in its silver-gray cover, as if quietly attempting to deflect any thought of the riches its little volume might contain (as if it wanted you to think it was hollow, or else solid plastic), was the "doorway" I referred to earlier: the desktop computer.

I removed the cover and plugged the cord into the wall.

Just as I find it hard to lie, so I dislike any form of prying or underhandedness. But I felt what I was doing was an instance of justifiable investigation: there was a question of intrusion here, after all. Besides which, by looking into it myself, I believed I might actually end up *protecting* my secret roommate (if indeed that was what he should turn out to be) from the presumably less desirable scrutiny of an official investigation, which was surely what awaited him if his illegal occupancy of this room continued for much longer.

I pressed the power button. The screen lit up with a little musical flourish, yielding its contents for my inspection. These were few in number and fewer still were of any obvious interest. Having become a fairly adept user of these machines, I was able to determine quite quickly that there was in fact only one document worth reading through. This was a lengthy, unfinished narrative about a man by the name of Kadmilos. Arriving in New York from an obscure, unnamed nation, this Kadmilos becomes infatuated with what he calls the "magnificent callousness" of the city, decides at all costs to stay, marries a woman for a green card, and embarks on the life of a cynical philanderer, wandering the streets and bars of Manhattan in search of women.

It was pretty clear to me that this was a piece of autobiographical fiction, with Kadmilos standing in for Trumilcik himself. There was a wearisome macho swagger in the tone that seemed entirely consistent with the image I had already formed of Trumilcik, and there was also the fact that for money, he (or his surrogate Kadmilos) taught at a college bearing a strong resemblance to Arthur Clay, toward whose female students he appeared to have the attitude of a sultan toward his private harem.

It wasn't a particularly edifying story, and in the end offered little clue to its author's present whereabouts. The only things that gave it any interest (and even that purely incidental) were one or two odd points of convergence between Kadmilos/Trumilcik's life in New York and my own. He lived for a time in the West Village, in the meatpacking district, as Carol and I had before moving across town. Reading his stiff but strangely vivid English, I had the feeling of being right back there on Horatio Street where beef carcasses were rolled out of trucks every morning on hangers like bloody dresses and blood froze in the cobbled gutters. Glimpses of pale partygoers breakfasting at Florent came back to me on a fond current of memory; Bolivian flowermen trimming dyed carnations outside the Korean groceries on Greenwich Avenue . . .

At one point, about halfway through, there was a prolonged scene down at the INS building on Federal Plaza, where, like me, the author had spent many hours waiting on line to fill out the multitude of elaborate forms required to obtain a visa.

I found this passage peculiarly absorbing. I see myself there in Room 106, hunched at the screen, mesmerized by the strange familiarity of it all. There, as I try to reconstruct it now, is the line of immigrants, already long at eight A.M., two hours before the building opens; the Latin Americans stocky and dark, wearing their poverty with a stoical air; the East Europeans with their penchant for zipper-slashed anoraks, their impatient look of having been kept *unjustly* poor. Here is the sour coffee you buy from the little stall as you join the line—run by a beaming couple who've just this moment, it would seem, tumbled out of the very mill you yourself are about to enter. Here are the security guards who man the metal detectors at the entrance and frisk you with their rubber-gloved hands. Kadmilos notes a merry lack of conviction in the way these young men, with their ear studs and clubland haircuts, wear their uniforms, and I find myself smiling in recognition. Passing through security, thirty of us are shepherded into a large room with doors that close automatically, whereupon the room turns out, lo, to be an elevator, rising slowly to a high floor where we find ourselves in a vast open prairie of a room with rows and rows of fixed orange seats surrounded by little glassed-off booths, each containing, like an egg its embryo, an immigration official. At one of these, when our number finally flashes up, we give our signature. Kadmilos remembers how, in his excitement, his hand shook, so that his official signature has a stumble in it. Mine had shaken too! He describes tapping his right index finger into fingerprint ink, then pressing it into the box on the form, gladdened at the thought of this inimitable detail of his existence entering the consciousness of the federal government. He remembers how, without explanation, the official then handed him a small sachet marked BENZALKONIUM CHLORIDE, how he opened it, mystified, to find a towelette inside, and realized it was for cleaning his finger, and had to choke back tears of joy at this marvelous grace note in the official procedure, noting merely as an added glory that the towelette doesn't actually remove the ink but simply smudges it all over his hand.

From there to the photograph line. The woman in front—dark-haired, elegant, discreetly coquettish in her yellow shawl—fusses with her hair: combing it, primping it, then pushing it back a little from her ears to reveal a pair of gold earrings. *Next!* calls the photographer. The woman sits in the metal chair, angling her neck so that her modest jewelry will catch the light. *Earrings!* the photographer yells, wagging an admonitory finger at her. She doesn't understand. *Aretes!* Embarrassed, she removes them at once, then stares crestfallen at the camera for her official mug shot.

While we wait for the photo I.D. to develop, we feel suddenly dizzy and nauseous. We realize it's the benzalkonium chloride on our fingers, possibly aided by an empty stomach and a sleepless night. Then our name is called; just our first name, Kadmilos remembers fondly, as though we are now on the most intimate, almost filial footing with the United States govern-

ment. And a moment later, there in our hand is our brown
Employment Authorization Card, with our little grainy photograph and our faltering signature.

Given what I discovered in my office the next morning, I should
add to this picture of me sitting there at Trumilcik's computer the
image of Trumilcik himself, watching me, for this turned out to
have been the case. Watching me, as it happens, from *inside* the
room itself.

I see him observing me with growing suspicion as I come to
the end of his document and without pause rise from my chair
to hook the computer up to the printer on the filing cabinet
across the room, evidently intending to print a copy of his narrative for myself and—who knows? (I imagine him thinking)—
take it home to plagiarize or otherwise misappropriate it. I
picture his relief as he sees that I can't find any printing paper in
the room and, with a glance at my train schedule, apparently
make up my mind to defer trying to print out his story until the
morning.

Exiting from the computer, I left the room, locking the door
behind me.

The night had cleared. The crisp, cool air was bracing.

Coming down Mulberry Street I saw a group of figures heading toward me. A little to my dismay (I'd have preferred not to
have had it known that I paid nocturnal visits to the campus),
they turned out to be Bruno's students, back from their play. The
two men, and three of the four women. They nodded at me as we
passed, and a few steps on I heard a snort of stifled laughter.

Down at the train station, I was about to pass through the
waiting room onto the platform when I heard the familiar voice
of Bruno himself, and stayed where I was; not intending to

snoop, just wanting to avoid an encounter that I realized would be awkward for us both.

He was with the fourth girl; the tall, waiflike one with blond hair. I'd seen her often on campus: a frail winter flower of a girl, wearing a tie-dye T-shirt in the snow. Bruno appeared to be in the process of trying to persuade her to return to New York with him.

Through the waiting room window I could see them in the powerful sodium lamp: Bruno leaning against an iron pillar, holding the girl's hands in his, the toplit smile of his boyish mouth shaping the words with languidly self-satisfied pouting movements, as if he were supremely confident of getting his way.

He spoke quietly, but his voice was one of those subtly rasping instruments that penetrate at even the lowest volumes, like a distant buzz saw or the purr of a cat.

"Don't send me home alone, Candy," he murmured. "Here, come here. . . ." He pulled her toward him, brushing her lips with his. She was taller than him; thin and frail in her denim jacket, her slim long legs in the thinnest of wool tights, one knee bent, the toe of her other foot swiveling in its suede ankle boot on the concrete floor, like the compass needle of her prevarication.

"I'm not sure," I heard her say, averting her head, though leaving her hands in his. "I'm not sure that would be such a great idea."

He pulled her back. Something—his slightly abnormal shortness, I suppose—made me suddenly think that, like many people who abuse their power over others, he had carried into adulthood some ancient sense of himself as a victim. I felt certain that he saw himself as the weaker party here; entitled—even obliged—to use any weapon he could: that he wasn't so much trying to possess the girl as conducting an ongoing act of defiance against the hand nature had dealt him as a physical specimen; a hand that appeared to have ruled beauty of the order this girl possessed forever out of reach. But although I sympathized with him for this, I held him entirely responsible for what he was doing. The girl's lips parted for another half-kiss. Seeing this—practiced manipulator that he evidently was—Bruno said flatly, "Okay, if that's what you think . . ." and let go of her hands. She stared at him, biting her lip, her eyes wide like a disappointed child's. He looked back at her, surer than ever, I felt, of his ground; making his own eyes glint in what seemed to me a downright predatory manner. One could practically see the look travel down through the girl's dilated pupils and spread out in a ramifying flush through the capillaries of her underdefended flesh.

The steel tracks gave a knife-grinding sound, and I could hear the distant roar of our approaching train.

"Night-night, then," Bruno said.

I was hoping they would move so I could come out without being seen, but they stayed there looking at each other, and as the train came hissing in, Bruno put a single finger under the girl's chin and brought her face down toward his. She had her hands in her pockets now, and as she let herself be tipped toward him, the effect was like that of seeing a delicate statue about to topple over. I felt that she was using the small range of gestures available to her at that moment to signal acquiescence, but of the most passive kind: *You've overpowered me*, she might have been saying. *I hereby inform you I no longer have any responsibility for my actions*.

The train doors had opened, and since the two of them were now locked in a kiss and making no move to get aboard, I had no choice but to come out of my hiding place in full view of Bruno; evidently not a man to kiss with his eyes closed. He saw me, of course, as I passed by, and I felt myself flinch as if it were I, not

he, who had been caught doing something questionable. I don't
know whether they boarded that train or stayed there smooching
till the next one came along.

As I rattled for the fourth time that day along the dirty creek,
my mind drifted in an abstract, speculative way over Trumilcik's
document.

I found myself thinking of the woman ahead of him on the
photograph line—the yellow-shawled woman he had described
as "coquettish." Catching up with her as he left the INS building
with his Employment Authorization Card, he had fallen into
conversation with her. As was often the case with him, the conversation had continued over the course of several nights at her
apartment, which was up on Central Park West, a block north of
the Dakota Building. The thought of their encounter seemed to
be offering some strange elegance of symmetry or reciprocity for
my enjoyment, but before my exhausted mind could grasp what
it was, I found myself suddenly remembering where I had seen
Blumfeld before.

Just before Carol left me, a colleague of hers had come to dinner, bringing her new girlfriend with her, an actress. After dinner,
the actress had suggested we all go to a club on Eleventh Avenue,
the Plymouth Rock, where sexual games of various kinds were
played. I had declined politely, explaining that I needed to be up
early the next morning for my employment authorization interview, the penultimate phase in my green card application procedure. I assumed that my wife, a medieval scholar not given to
caprices of a sexual or any other nature, would likewise decline.
To my astonishment, however, she had accepted, and insisted
on going even when I discreetly suggested she may have drunk
more than she realized. She left me at home with the dishes, and
the strange sense of being a spoilsport, something I had never
before suspected her of thinking.

The actress was Blumfeld. He was a woman! Hence those hairless white hands; hence that secretive, mischievous look in her eyes. . . .

I arrived home still absorbed in this discovery—so much so that I forgot to avoid looking at the answering machine on my way through the living room and found myself stalled by the unexpected pulsation of a red light.

I allowed myself a moment of joy as I watched it flashing. Then, as I always did on the rare occasions when the machine held a message for me, I deleted it without listening to it, so as not to risk the disappointment of it not being from Carol.

Chapter 3

The next morning I took the train back to work with a fresh sheaf of laser printer paper in my briefcase. I wanted to print out Trumilcik's manuscript and reread it; that was all.

That *was* all, though I should say that although I had never had any literary ambitions of my own, I had recently read several articles about the colossal advances being paid to novelists, and as a result had briefly included novel-writing among the various alternative career fantasies I drifted into whenever I found myself worrying about money. I had even gone so far as to embark on a little story—it was called *S for Salmon*—to see if I had any talent for invention. I hadn't been pleased with the results, and that particular daydream had faded from the roster.

I mention this purely to play devil's advocate against myself; to make the case that if Trumilcik had been able to see inside my head and piece together the frailest remains of buried wishes, he might indeed have been justified in regarding me as a would-be plagiarist, though even then he would have been wrong. As it is,

I can only attribute his subsequent actions to an innate suspiciousness bordering on paranoia.

My office was as I had left it. I closed the door behind me and took the fat sheaf of paper from my bag, tearing off its wrapper and loading the pristine white block into the printer. Removing the cover from the computer, I pressed the power button, watched the screen flicker on, heard the tinny synthetic fanfare, gave the list-files command, and saw with the kind of pang you feel when a blissful encounter evaporates as you wake and realize you were merely dreaming it, that the document was no longer there.

After repeating the operation, checking the recycle bin, and trying out every other exploring and resuscitating technique I knew, I had no choice but to acknowledge the fact that I had been observed last night, presumably by Trumilcik himself.

My first thought was that he must have been on his way into the office, perhaps to continue working on this very document, when he had noticed the light on and had crept up to the window, watching me through the latticed panes as I devoured his story. If this were the case, he would have had to be standing close to the window itself, somewhere in the patch of ground defined by the flying buttresses that protruded from either side of the casement and a line of thick, eight-foot-high hemlocks running parallel with the wall. The room wouldn't have been clearly visible from beyond this small oblong. Not being a walkway, the area had held its patch of old snow more or less intact, and had anyway been completely covered with new snow from the flurries that had fallen before I arrived last night. Anyone standing there watching me would have left footprints, but there were no footprints.

I was reluctant to proceed from there to the next logical step: that I had been observed from within the room. Aside from everything else, it seemed a practical impossibility that a second person could have been in the room all the time I was there; unheard, unseen, unsuspected even, by me. For form's sake, more than out of any conviction that Trumilcik could have been hiding in there, I opened the little storage closet where I had seen the air conditioner and Barbara Hellermann's clothes. The space showed no obvious sign of intrusion, and I saw that even if someone had been in there with the door ajar, they would have seen nothing but a thin strip of wall with the owl-face of a light switch and the piece of paper with the quotation from Louisa May Alcott. Anyway, if there really was someone frequenting the room on a clandestine basis, they would surely have had to come up with a less obvious way of concealing themselves, should the need to do so arise, than a closet.

But the fact remained that the document, which had been in the computer less than twelve hours before, was no longer there, and that even if I had *not* been observed reading it, someone had been in the room between my leaving it last night and returning this morning.

Uncertain what to make of any of this, I left to teach my class. We were reading the *Bacchae*, with a view to seeing whether Pentheus, the "chilly" opponent (and victim) of Dionysus, might be reclaimable as a prototype for a new kind of male hero. An interesting discussion arose on the death-walk sequence in the last act, where Pentheus, apparently mad, puts on women's clothing and sets off for what turns out to be his own violent destruction. I remember that several of us discerned an undertow of something dignified, almost majestic in his behavior, counteracting the framing tone of mockery and humiliation cast by the triumphantly scornful Dionysus, as though, at the point of delivering on its hackneyed message about not offending the gods, the play had inadvertently stumbled on some larger, deeper truth about the tyranny of the supposedly "natural" laws of gender and was surreptitiously offering Pentheus as a martyr figure in the struggle against this tyranny. At any rate, it was a good class, lively and stimulating, and I left it feeling mildly elated.

From there I went to have lunch. I was carrying my tray to one of the small tables by the window (I usually sat by myself in the faculty dining room) when I caught sight of a woman looking up at me from a table in the corner of the room. It took me a moment to realize that it was Elaine Jordan, the school attorney. She had had her hair set in a new way, and in contrast to her usual self-effacing outfits of shapeless acrylic, she was wearing a tailored jacket and skirt with a frilled silk blouse.

I was about to nod and continue on when I noticed something tentatively solicitous about her look, as though she were hoping I would eat at her table. I moved in her direction, and saw that this was in fact the case. Her expression grew more openly welcoming as I approached, and when I asked if I could join her, she replied with a wordless, intent smile. I smiled back at her, feeling vaguely under an obligation to match her intensity.

"So," she said after a moment, "here you are."

"Yes."

Another exchange of smiles followed. I busied myself for a moment arranging my lunch on the table. I hadn't eaten with Elaine before; had had almost no contact with her, in fact, other than at the weekly meetings of our committee. She wasn't the kind of person who makes much of an impression on you—nothing obviously striking about her personality or looks to stall your thoughts or draw them back to her after she was out of your immediate orbit. As with Dr. Schrever, I wouldn't have been able to say how old she was, what color her eyes were, what shade of brown her hair was, without looking at her. I didn't have an opinion of her, I suppose, because at some level I didn't consider her a person of whom I needed to form an opinion. I wondered now if perhaps she had perceived this indifference (it amounted to that) and, in the gently insistent way of certain meek but not after all entirely self-abnegating spirits, had summoned me over to her table in order, ever so gently, to reprove me for this: to make me acknowledge her as a human being, not merely a part of the administrative machinery.

I felt immediately chastened by this thought, as though I had been guilty of downright disrespect, and I was eager to show my willingness to make amends. I presumed this would take the form of having her talk to me at length about herself.

"How's your work going?" I asked, attempting to get the ball rolling right away.

"Good. And yours?"

"Fine. But what are you—what have you been doing?"

"Oh—not much. Surviving! How about you?"

There was an odd intensity, still, in her look, that made me wonder whether I had in fact appraised the situation correctly. She seemed nervous but at the same time oddly exuberant—triumphant almost. She patted her hair nervously; adjusted the collar of her tailored jacket—charcoal, with thin turquoise stripes—wafting a billow of surprisingly sweet perfume in my direction.

"Not a lot," I said. "Waiting for winter to end."

We both chuckled loudly, as if there were something hilarious about that. Then there was another drawn-out silence. Elaine looked down at the table. She was smiling oddly to herself, perhaps debating whether or not to say something that was on her mind. Then, flashing her eyes candidly up at me, she said softly:

"I'm glad you came, Lawrence."

I was a little startled by that. I didn't want to believe what my instincts were beginning to tell me, but in case they were correct I felt I should do something to neutralize the situation as quickly as possible. To buy time, I filled my mouth with food and began thinking furiously of something to say, but my mind was an absolute blank.

By luck, Roger Freeman, the head of our committee, appeared at our table just then.

"Greetings," he said.

He sat down, unloading his tray with the ease of a man who feels welcome wherever he goes. Glancing at Elaine, he evidently took in the change in her appearance. For a moment he seemed to be considering the propriety of commenting on it. I assumed he would suppress the impulse, as I had, but to my surprise he spread a cheerful smile across his face.

"That's a new hairstyle. It suits you." He turned to me: "Don't you agree, Lawrence?"

"Yes, it's very nice."

Elaine thanked us with a little ironic swipe at her hair, and we all laughed.

As we conversed, it struck me that there had been something deliberate and self-conscious about Roger's remark. Almost as if, by saying something that in another man might have sounded questionable, he was demonstrating his consummate probity; showing that he possessed, *in himself,* some purifying quality that could render any wrong word or gesture innocent merely by virtue of the fact that *he* was its instrument of expression. I felt how much of a piece with this probity all his other qualities were—his dapperness, his cheerful, sparkling eye, the healthy flush of his wrinkled face. The fanciful idea came to me that *anything* he did would so thoroughly partake of this wholesomeness that, even if he were to do something on the face of it utterly crass or gross, such as sliding his hand up Elaine's skirt, the action would become instantly so blameless that nobody would bat an eyelid.

"Anyway," he continued, lowering his voice, "on a more press-ing note: we need to meet again A.S.A.P. I've told the others. There's been a formal complaint about—about the person we were discussing last time. I'll give you the details when we meet. Any chance you could make it on Monday afternoon, Lawrence? Is that one of your days?"

It would mean canceling Dr. Schrever—a hundred bucks down the drain unless she could reschedule, which she usually couldn't.

"It's rather urgent," Roger prompted me.

"That's fine," I said, "no problem."

"Good."

In the pause that followed, Elaine glanced at me, lightly curv-ing the corners of her lips in what seemed to be a look of secret solidarity.

"Roger, who is this Trumilcik guy?" I heard myself ask. "You mentioned him at the last meeting."

"Trumilcik! Oh, boy . . ."

After repeating what I had already learned from Marsha, he embarked on one of his concise, *précis*-like appraisals of the case. Though I was naturally interested, I was somewhat dis-tracted by the continuing oddness of Elaine's demeanor, and I remember little about what Roger said other than that it left me feeling not much the wiser as far as Trumilcik was concerned.

"Part of it undoubtedly was that he came from a different cul-ture," Roger concluded, "with a different set of values, and we worked hard to make allowances for that, didn't we, Elaine?"

"Did we ever!" Elaine assented, dutifully rolling her eyes, though I could tell she wasn't remotely interested in the discus-sion. Her gaze returned to me; rather wistfully now, I thought.

"What happened to him after he left?" I asked.

"I don't know. He had a wife, if you can believe it, someone he met over here, though I think she'd already thrown him out by the time this all erupted. How come you're interested?"

"Just curious."

I had noticed him glancing over at the clock as he spoke. Not wanting to risk being left alone with Elaine again, I hurried down my lunch and made my excuses.

In my building, as I headed back to my room, I heard my name called. I turned to see Amber, the graduate intern, standing in the corridor behind me.

"Hi," I said, keeping my distance.

"I was wondering if I could ask you a big favor. . . ."

As always, her presence, somnolent-eyed yet keenly projected into the space about her, unnerved me.

"Of course."

"Would you mind reading something I've written? It's sort of in your field. . . ."

In the fluorescent light of the corridor her shorn orange hair and gold-freckled, bluish white skin had an unnatural, pallid luminosity. Her awkwardness seemed genuine enough, but it didn't diminish the impression of fundamental poise and confidence underlying it. She seemed to proffer the chalice of herself with a strange, innocent blatancy. As a male in a position of power, one had to be vigilant over the inclination of one's eye to stray at these moments, or the tendency of one's voice to convey impulses unconnected to the ostensible matter at hand. And as a member of the Sexual Harassment Committee, I was doubly aware of the need for this vigilance. Out of the mass of mental events that occurred during exchanges such as this, only a very few were admissible into the field of acknowledged reality. The rest constituted a kind of vast, unauthorized apocrypha.

"Sure," I said. "Just put it in my box."

She thanked me, and I continued on my way, reflexively

checking over what I had said for any unintended innuendo, and concluding that I had nothing to worry about.

Back in my office I found myself once again puzzling about the disappearance of Trumilcik's document. As I looked at the computer on its cumbrous desk, I was struck for the first time by the arrangement of furniture in that part of the room. The two oversized desks had been pushed together in such a way as to contain, I realized now, an enclosed space at their center. How large it might be I couldn't tell from the outside, but I was suddenly curious.

I went over and pulled at one of the desks. Nothing budged at first, and it wasn't until I heaved at it with all my strength, bracing my foot against a raised rib on the side of the other desk, that I was able to slide it a few inches. I peered in through the gap: there did seem to be a sizable space in there. I prized the desks far enough apart to squeeze inside.

The moment I was in there, I had the sense of having entered a human habitation. It was perhaps five feet square, not more than three feet high. Balled up on one side was something soft that, as I held it out in the light, turned out to be a sheet. It was stained, stiffened in parts by paint and God knows what other substances. As I shook it open, it gave off a staleness that seemed to me unmistakably male. Something else fell out of it; hard and heavy: a metal rod about fifteen inches long, with a thread at one end, as though perhaps it had formed part of the construction of the desk; some sort of ferrule or reinforcing rod.

I sat there, hunched and strangely excited, my heart beating hard in my chest. Was it possible that Trumilcik had been sitting here, silent and immobile, all the time I was here last night? Against the improbability of that conjecture was the distinct, palpable human atmosphere of the place—something acrid, masculine, faintly derelict.

To get a better sense of how he would have felt if he *had* been there, I grasped an inner strut on the desk I had shifted and, with a mighty effort, managed to close myself in.

It was dark, but not quite pitch-black: ahead of me at eye level was a slit of light, about three feet long and a third of an inch wide, where someone had apparently forced open a gap in the joint between the side wall of the desk and its overhanging surface. Through it I could see a thin cross section of the room, which included part of a bookshelf and most of the wall with the door. I couldn't see the printer, but I could see a strip of the cabinet it was sitting on, so that I would have seen the middle six inches of my body had I been sitting there spying on myself last night, and would certainly have guessed that I was doing something with the printer.

I could see in its entirety the bowl full of bits and pieces where I had found the Bulgarian coin, and the disturbing thought struck me that it was perhaps not just last night that Trumilcik had sat there in secret observing me, but on other occasions too; numerous, perhaps, but even if not, requiring a reappraisal of my entire sense of my occupancy of this office: an acknowledgment that at any given moment as I went about my business, imagining I was alone there, I might in fact have been under close and—I sensed—not especially friendly scrutiny.

I thought of the things Trumilcik might have seen or heard me do, and tried to observe myself doing them from his point of view. Two hours a week were set aside for conferences with individual students. Since I made these occasions as public and impersonal as possible, keeping the door open in accordance with Elaine's recommendations, I doubted whether Trumilcik would have seen anything to interest him. More disturbing was the thought of him overhearing some of the things I might have said aloud in private, particularly during the phone calls I had made at the beginning of term, before I broke myself of the habit. These were calls to my own machine at home; silent hangups initially, made simply so that I wouldn't have to return to a nonflashing machine (I would delete all messages without listening, as I still did), but then, for a period, consisting of little friendly messages to myself, first from me, but then, as the sense of the need to inhibit myself in what I took to be an entirely private act diminished, from Carol—my imitation of her crisp phrasing and intonation, if not her actual voice—telling me she loved me, begging me to return her calls, until I realized this was not a particularly healthy thing to be doing, and I stopped. What would Trumilcik have made of those calls, I wondered uneasily, if he had heard them?

As I squatted there in the near-darkness of his hiding place, I heard a knock at the door.

I didn't want whoever it was to hear me call out "Come in" in a mysteriously muffled voice, only to find me emerging from under the desk as they opened the door. Nor did I want my invitation to come in to be preceded by a hurried shifting of furniture, so I said nothing at all and waited for the person to go away. But instead of retreating footsteps, I heard another knock. Again I said nothing. The strip of door I could see through my slit contained the handle, and to my dismay I now saw the handle turn and the door begin to open.

A figure slipped in, leaving the door behind it ajar. All I could see was a section of waist and hip, but they were covered in a material of gray wool with turquoise pinstripes that I recognized immediately as Elaine's. What on earth was she doing? I sat frozen at the slit, my eyes wide open, my heart pounding. She started moving about the room; looking at things, I supposed, checking out the books, objects, pictures, the way you do in someone else's office. All the while she was humming to herself—

a tuneless but jaunty drone, as if she were feeling on top of the world. I saw her hips cross back from the shelves to the side of the door, where she paused and after a moment stopped humming too. She must have been reading the quotation from Louisa May Alcott. She gave a long, pleased-sounding *hmmm*. Then, smoothing her skirt over her behind, she moved on, disappearing from view.

For the first time now I noticed a number of small, unobtrusive mirrors, placed here and there in my field of vision. I couldn't see much in them, but they had evidently been positioned to pick up movement in any corner of the room, so that although I could no longer see Elaine, I could tell that she had crossed to my own desk and was now standing still—presumably examining its surface. After a moment she crossed back and sat down in the swivel chair I kept for students, turning around in it, so that her thighs and knees suddenly swung directly into my line of vision, about four feet from my face.

What a stupendously odd situation to find myself in! I felt what it must be like to wear a chador, a yashmak; to go about the world revealing nothing of yourself, and seeing only the equivalent of this truncated strip of Elaine's midriff. And continuing the line of thought I had been pursuing just a few minutes earlier, I was struck by the notion that this state of affairs wasn't after all so different from the normal manner in which men like myself were getting accustomed to conducting our relations with other people; either totally concealing ourselves, or else revealing only what we ourselves hadn't yet deemed inadmissible in civilized discourse; an aperture no less narrow than the one I was presently peeping through, and getting thinner by the day, so that all one ever really acknowledged of another person was the equivalent of what I was looking at now. Elaine's hand flashed across the bar of light, sweeping over her skirt-tightened thigh and into her lap. The still-visible wrist it was attached to began moving, working busily from side to side. The knee crossed over its twin with a light fall of drapery that exposed a thin, iridescent slip under the skirt. After a while she stood up, going once more to my desk.

I heard some squirting sounds I couldn't decipher. A moment later she reappeared by the door and left, closing it behind her.

I waited several minutes before I dared move. When I did, I found I was soaked through with sweat. I also appeared to have been clutching the metal bar all this time—so tightly the muscles in my hand had all but frozen themselves onto it.

As I stepped out into the room, I realized what the squirting sounds had been: Elaine had sprayed the place with her lemony-sugary perfume. I saw too what she had been doing in the swivel chair: writing a note. It lay on my desk, folded over with my name on the outside in large, round letters. I picked it up and unfolded it: *Why oh why,* it read, *did Roger have to show up like that? We do seem to be star-crossed! Anyway, this little note is to tell you I'm sorry it didn't go as planned, but we do have all the time in the world after all, and I'm in your room at least, my gentle friend, drinking in the sight of your things (so you, those cups, so funny and original!) And that beautiful quotation on the wall: it made me feel almost as good about what I did last night as I do about you showing up at lunch like that in your shirt. Anyway I've got to run now, so if I don't catch you later I'll call you tonight. Till then . . . ??Darling?? . . . Elaine.*

This seemed to indicate a new depth of strangeness. What lunacy could have possessed such a sensible-seeming woman to behave like this? The thing that made it peculiarly disturbing was the way she appeared to have hallucinated my acquiescence in her fantastical scenario.

I went home; confused and distantly alarmed.

My apartment felt oppressively empty. When Carol left, she took with her every shred of evidence connecting us, from the furniture and the kitchen stuff she'd brought with her, to our wedding photo from City Hall.

Bereft of her, the place had languished. Piles of dusty papers and clothes grew over the floor and furniture. As soon as I cleared one up, another would appear somewhere else: apparently I was intent on creating disorder behind my own back. Sometimes, though, the rooms seemed to fill with a ghostly memory of her. The staleness would go from the air. The bookshelves would seem crowded again with her books on medieval art and thought. I would have the distinct sense that if I were to open the bedroom closet in such a way as to catch it unawares, her side of it would be filled again with her clothes; the neatly folded piles cool and soft, scented with the fragrance that was not so much the residue of a soap or perfume as the emanation of a fine and pure spirit.

I went into the kitchen; thought of cooking a meal, then decided not to. I wandered back into the living room; picked up a sweater from a stack of things on a recessed ledge beside the sofa. . . . Under it lay some printed pages. A phrase caught my eye: *Elaine's pale breasts and thighs* . . . Amazed, I picked up the pages. They were the typescript of the story I had tried to write a few months ago—*S for Salmon*. I'd forgotten I had used the name Elaine.

The story was about a man having an affair. Returning to his office after a lunchtime assignation with his mistress, he finds a message from his wife asking him to bring home a wild salmon from the nearby fishmonger. He goes there right away to be sure of getting one before they run out. It's a hot day; the office fridge turns out to be too small to accommodate the big fish, so he takes it down to the storage room, the only cool place in the building. Seeing a glue-trap covered in cockroaches, he puts the fish in a metal filing cabinet, selecting the s–z drawer. Later, he leaves the office, hurrying to get the train his wife's expecting him on. Only as he pulls out of the station does he realize he has left the fish behind in the filing cabinet. It's a Friday; the office is locked all weekend. The story ends with him on the train, guiltily picturing the fish—a beautiful, rainbow-mailed creature with dark pink flesh in its slit belly—dulling and decomposing in its metal tomb, while insects swarm over the cabinet, trying to get inside.

The line that had caught my eye came from the assignation at the beginning, where the man and his mistress are making love in a hotel room. Apparently I had named the mistress Elaine.

In the light of what had happened today, I had to wonder if there was any significance in this. Bearing in mind what I had learned in my sessions with Dr. Schrever, I tried to think what the name had meant to me when I chose it. Had I been thinking of Elaine Jordan? If so, was that because I had placed her, unconsciously, in the category of plausible sexual partner? And if that were the case, had I perhaps all this time been emitting signals of sexual interest in her, without knowing it—signals that had become transformed, in her inflamed imagination, into the sense of an actual, ongoing liaison between us? And if all this were so, did that mean that under the complete indifference I believed I felt toward her, I did in fact harbor feelings of desire?

As I was turning this over in my mind, Mr. Kurwen's first TV came on. A moment later I heard the second, even louder than the first. There was a new level of assault in the volume; a suggestion of deliberate affront. I decided to go up and complain.

This time Mr. Kurwen's glass eye was out. The white-lashed pucker of the eyelid over the empty socket struck me nearly dumb. Flakes of dried food fluttered at his mouth, impaled on his white stubble. A fetid stench reared up out of the hallway behind him. He scanned me aggressively with his good eye, then, to my surprise, gave me a rueful smile.

"Better late than never. C'mon in." *C'mawn* . . . He had the old-time New York accent; a rarity in Manhattan these days. The lap-dogs yapped at his heels.

As he ushered me in, I felt his hand tousling my hair. I looked back, astonished.

"Go on, go on," he said gruffly, waving me on into the living room. There was a gold carpet; thick floral curtains. The smell—canine, human, with a tinge of something absolutely unearthly too—was so intense I felt myself gagging. The heat was over-powering too. And the TV, dueling with its partner in the adjoining bedroom, filled the place with an earsplitting din.

"Fix yourself a drink." He pointed at a cabinet where an assortment of ancient bottles presided over some dusty cut-glass tumblers.

I shook my head. "The TVs," I said. "Do you think you could turn them down?"

He cupped a hand to his ear.

"The TVs!" I bellowed.

He gave a guilty, impish grin, fumbling for the volume knob and turning it down.

"I turn 'em up loud just to keep the little prick downstairs on his toes," he said, going off to turn down the one in the bedroom.

A pang of hurt went through me at that. Not that I had any reason to care what this old man thought of me. But the only real news you ever get of yourself is what comes inadvertently from other people.

I was curious who he thought I was, if not the "prick down-stairs."

"Anyways," he said, returning, "I think it's in the kitchen somewhere."

"What is?"

"My eye. That's where I last had it. I was boiling it in the pan. I must've put it somewheres by accident."

I got the idea that whoever I was, I was expected to go in the kitchen and look for the missing eye. I went in there, leaving the other eye staring at a laxative commercial on the TV.

The kitchen floor was sticky with grime; I felt like a fly walking on flypaper. I saw the eye right away, staring up at me from under an old cupboard on which the green paint had broken down into a mosaic of tiny hard blobs. The eye was the size of a golf ball. I picked it up, meaning to give it to Mr. Kurwen, when I decided to pocket it instead. I was vaguely thinking it might come in useful later on, as leverage over the TVs.

"What is it with the guy downstairs?" I called out.

"He's a prick."

"But in what way?" I went back into the living room, looking squarely at Mr. Kurwen.

"Whaddaya mean, in what way? He's a prick! Mimi talked to the wife the day she moved out on him. She told me the guy had to've been a total prick."

"What exactly did she say about him—the wife?"

"What is this, a Q and A? How the fuck would I know what she said?"

"I thought—"

But all of a sudden I felt tired of the deception. I had an overwhelming desire to reveal myself to the old man; to come out, as it were, from under my desk.

"Listen," I told him, "I'm not who you think I am."

He peered at me, not understanding at first, then disbelieving, then angry, with a pale flame of old man's fear wavering over the anger.

"What is this?"

"I'm the guy downstairs. The prick downstairs. I just came up to complain about the noise of your TVs. You must have been expecting someone else, right?"

"You're not Corven?"

"No, I'm not Corven."

He looked at me mistrustfully. "I don't see so good no more," he muttered.

"I'm sorry about that."

"Diabetes."

"Ah."

"On top of my wife dying I have to become a fucking diabetic."

"That's rough. I'm sorry."

He stood there in the doorway, the light glinting around the stubbly perimeter of his face, while I made my way through the hallway, where the airless, lightless space squeezed the stench and heat to a suffocating intensity.

"So would you mind keeping the volume down?" I asked, turning back to him from the front door.

He grimaced. His swaggerer's courage had returned to him now that he saw I was going to leave without beating him to a pulp.

"I'll think about it," he said nastily, but then took a frightened step back.

"It would make a huge difference to me, Mr. Kurwen, really."

His face went abruptly slack. He turned and hobbled away, an old man, saying nothing.

I left, depressed by him, but glad of the plain-dealing way in which I had acquitted myself. It gave me a pleasant feeling of large-spiritedness.

Back downtairs I read the phrase that had caught my eye again: *Elaine's pale breasts and thighs* . . . I realized I had pictured my protagonist's mistress in the most stereotypical terms;

as a torso without occupation, personality or history: just an embodiment of the idea of lustful infidelity. What if I were to model her on the real Elaine, I wondered; would that bring this stillborn effort to life? But how would I convey the real Elaine— the transcendent ordinariness she projected, even in the midst of her bizarre behavior today? And if I succeeded, how then would I account for the man's attraction to her? He didn't have much personality either, come to think of it. He didn't even have a name. In the terse style I had opted for, I referred to him merely as "he." I decided there and then to name him. I picked up a pen, crossed out the first "he," and with a feeling of amusement, replaced it with the word "Kadmilos."

At once something seemed to stir in the sheaf of pages; a little quiver of life. . . . With Kadmilos/Trumilcik in play, the figure of Elaine suddenly seemed capable of making the transition from erotic projection to flesh and blood. Furthermore, conceived as the real Elaine, but looked at through the eyes of Kadmilos, her very ordinariness acquired a sudden allure.

I thought of the three of us—myself, Trumilcik, and Elaine— each present there via our more or less phantasmagorical versions of each other, our recondite emblems of ourselves. And for a moment I felt I was at the point of grasping what it was that made the full unfolding of another human being into one's consciousness so painfully dazzling that one spent one's life contriving ways of filtering them, blocking them out, setting up labyrinthine passageways between oneself and them, kidnapping their images for various exploitative purposes of one's own, and generally doing all one could to fend off their problematic, objective reality.

The phone rang.

I let the machine pick up. Elaine's voice came into the room.

"Hi, there, me again. Guess I missed you. I hope you got my

note. Well . . ." She sounded a bit forlorn, but then went on in a firmer tone. "Call me, would you, Lawrence, when you get in? Doesn't matter how late." She left her number and hung up.

It was only now that I thought of the message I had erased the previous night without listening to it. I realized that it had probably been from Elaine. I tried to surmise what she could have said, and how I could have unwittingly responded to it in such a way as to unleash the delusionary behavior that followed.

At once I remembered the phrase in her note about me turning up at lunch *like that in your shirt*. An idea began taking shape in my mind. It was absurd, I realized, as its outlines clarified themselves, and yet there was a certain mad logic about it that didn't seem out of keeping with the side of her personality Elaine had displayed this afternoon.

She had made some kind of wild declaration of love, I conjectured, followed by a proposal that if I reciprocated her feelings, I should indicate the fact by joining her for lunch dressed in a particular shirt—presumably the very one I happened to be wearing.

What an elaborate rigmarole! And yet I found I could imagine her doing all this. Suppose she had been attracted to me for some time, I thought; suppose I had unconsciously been giving her encouraging signals; suppose then that her feelings had grown to such passionate proportions that she simply had to confront me with them so as to break the deadlock of what, from her point of view, might have seemed an agonizingly slow-burning flirtation that was in danger of missing its moment if one of us didn't act soon. With the enormous courage it must have taken for a woman who presumably wasn't excessively confident of her own attractiveness, she had crossed the Rubicon of natural inhibition and blurted out her feelings onto my answering machine, risking the pain of a rebuff, from which she had touchingly tried to protect both of us by asking me to give my answer in a manner that would allow the misunderstanding, if that was what it turned out to be, to sink into the oblivion of history without any echoing residue of words to keep its memory alive. I was just to show up wearing a certain shirt.

I thought of how she must have felt sitting there in the faculty dining room, anxiously waiting, unsure perhaps of her choice of outfit, her new hairdo; a little dazed, still, by what she had done, yet elated by it, carried forward by the momentum of her liberated passion, looking at her watch, thinking that at the very worst she would have a story to tell her grandchildren if she were lucky enough—*blessed* enough—to have any, and then looking up to see, as if in a vision, me, walking uncertainly toward her in my black-buttoned blue shirt, a blue wave of love, rippling through her with the miraculous force of an answered prayer. . . .

Such are the phantoms we create out of each other. And although as phantoms went it was an improvement on the "prick downstairs," the idea of it left me with the same sense of depleted reality, as though I had been improperly replicated, and grown correspondingly lighter and flimsier in myself. No wonder, I thought, that so many people end up feeling like the human equivalent of a Bulgarian coin.

Chapter 4

"Before we start, I'd like you to take a look at something."

I felt a stirring in the air behind me, then a disturbance in my field of vision as Dr. Schrever's hand crossed over my prone head, holding a small piece of paper. My heart gave an unaccountable little thump.

The piece of paper was a check. I had signed and mailed it to her the day before.

"Do you notice something strange about it?" she asked.

Had I signed someone else's name? No; the signature looked all right, unless I was truly going out of my mind. The amount was the same as I always made out the checks for. And the date looked right too.

"What's wrong with it?" I asked.

"You can't see?"

"No."

"Look who it's made out to."

I saw then that I had made the check out to a Dr. *Schroeder* instead of Dr. Schrever. The error made me laugh out loud.

"Why did I do that?"

"Why do you think you did it?"

"I have absolutely no idea!"

"Do you know somebody called Schroeder?"

"Not that I can think of."

"A student of yours, perhaps?"

"No."

"Someone from England?"

I couldn't think of anyone by that name.

"I wonder why it made you laugh when you saw it?"

"I suppose there's something inherently comical about these little slips."

"I'm wondering if you laughed because you recognized some hostility you felt towards me, that embarrasses you to have to acknowledge?"

I told her I didn't think this was so; she didn't pursue the point. I corrected the check and returned it to her.

I had come in thinking I was going to talk about Elaine, but something had snagged on the current of my thoughts, drawing them in another direction. After a moment I realized what it was.

"When you moved your hand over my head just now, I felt myself flinching. I must have thought for a moment that you were going to tousle my hair. My stepfather used to do that. It was his one sign of affection. . . ."

While I was talking I remembered how Mr. Kurwen had tousled my hair last night as I went past him into his living room, and I realized that at the back of my mind I had been thinking about my childhood ever since then.

Instead of going on to talk about that, though, I interrupted myself to tell Dr. Schrever about my encounter with Mr. Kurwen;

how he had mistaken me for someone he'd asked to come and help find his glass eye, how in my dislike of confrontation I had half gone along with this error, but how I had then come clean to him instead, telling him he'd made a mistake, and asking him, in my capacity as the "prick downstairs," to keep his TV down.

I went on at some length about how large-spirited I had felt after this outburst of candor.

"Aside from tousling your hair," Dr. Schrever asked after a pause, "was there some other way this person made you think of your stepfather?"

"I guess I must have been wondering if he'd mistaken me for his son. Which is sort of the way I always felt about my stepfather. Unsure whether he thought of me as a son, unsure to what degree I *was* his son. . . ."

"Go on. . . ."

For a long time now, I had been aware of the gentle pressure of Dr. Schrever's professional interest, urging me to talk about my childhood. I had resisted for two reasons. First, I had no interest in being psychoanalyzed: I was seeing her for professional reasons of my own, namely that I was intending to write a book about gender relations in the evolution of psychoanalytic practice. My sources would mainly be memoirs and case histories, but I had felt that some firsthand experience would also be of value, to give me a sense of the particular textures of the exchange that takes place in these rooms. For obvious reasons I hadn't mentioned this motive to Dr. Schrever. Second, even though it was necessary for the purposes of my experiment to reveal certain things about myself to Dr. Schrever, even quite intimate things, I felt that she, as an American, simply wouldn't be able to understand the context in which my childhood had occurred. Certain obvious things I could explain, but there would be countless nuances I wouldn't even know I needed to explain, so that in all likelihood she would draw a series of entirely wrong conclusions about me.

How, for example, would she know that for a widowed, single mother to get herself badly in debt in order to send her only child away to boarding school at the age of eight was neither an unnatural nor an unloving act, but in the context of the niche of English society she aspired to occupy, the very opposite of those things? How could Dr. Schrever understand (or if she did, take seriously) the codes of speech and behavior by which each caste of that overcrowded island policed its boundaries; how violently offensive it had been, for instance, for my mother to refer to a napkin as a *serviette* in the presence of my stepfather's old schoolfriends, or say *pleased to meet you* when they were introduced, or stress the wrong syllable of *controversy*? And if she couldn't understand these things, how would she understand the intrinsic tensions and fault lines of our household; the peculiar fraught atmosphere bred by the very nature of its inception: the cultured and epicurean company directory with an aristocratic wife and three children at the ancestral manor, becoming steadily intoxicated with the charms of his new secretary; guiltily decanting the choice vintage of his existence from its nobly cellared and patinated bottle into the dubious, cut-price crystal of my mother's and mine?

It seemed a waste of time to broach the subject.

"What are you feeling, Lawrence?" I heard Dr. Schrever say.

"I'm feeling that I . . . that I didn't adequately express how good I felt about my straightforwardness with the old man upstairs. There was something about the simple, man-to-man way I ended up talking to him that made me feel almost . . . American."

"What does that mean to you, to feel American?"

"Released," I said. As I explained my view of America, that everything in it, from its architecture to its patterns of speech, was the expression of the single, simple sensation of release, the buzzer sounded, bringing the session to an end.

I stood up from the couch and went out through the small room where the next patient was waiting. I was just leaving the building when I heard Dr. Schrever's voice behind me.

"Lawrence, would you mind just stepping back in here for a moment?"

I went back into her room. She closed the door.

"You seem to have left something for me," she said, pointing at the couch.

There on the crimson corduroy lay Mr. Kurwen's glass eye.

I had forgotten this misdemeanor. The eye must have been in my pocket ever since I had picked it up from Mr. Kurwen's kitchen floor the night before.

Before I knew it—without even the usual warning—I began to turn the same color as Dr. Schrever's couch. She looked at me quizzically.

"I can explain—" I blustered, seeing her little notebook on the shelf by her chair.

"Perhaps next time?"

She picked the glass ball from the couch with the tips of her fingers and handed it back to me.

Outside it was clear and chilly. Sunlight glinted on the new snow bordering the paths into the park. It must have been warm enough to melt the top layer of flakes, as there was a smooth metallic crust over the surface. I found myself wandering in through one of the small entrances. Up through the trees the sky was a fabulous dark fluorescent blue. I stared at it for several blissful seconds. Looking back down, I saw the woman I had mistaken for Dr. Schrever. She was heading out of the park on a path that intersected with mine.

I looked hard, to make doubly sure it was her. Shortish dark hair, olive skin; that particular look of casual elegance . . . it was unmistakably her. She was wearing a long green coat with astrakhan collar and cuffs, and ankle boots trimmed with black fur or wool.

As she reached our intersection, crossing it ahead of me, I had a sudden urge to catch up with her and accost her. I quickened my pace. She must have been aware of me out of the corner of her eye. She turned and paused, looking directly at me. There under the eaves of her dark hair were two golden earrings. *Aretes!* I almost said the word aloud as I remembered the woman Trumilcik had met in the photograph line at the INS building. For she had lived, had she not, up here? A block north of the Dakota Building. . . . Smiling broadly, I walked on toward her. At that, with an abrupt tightening of her lips, she moved off; not running, but unmistakably hurrying away from me.

I stopped at once, realizing what she had taken me for. I had only wanted to ask her if by any chance she happened to be a friend of Bogomil Trumilcik and, if so, to talk to her about him, but obviously she couldn't have known that.

Even so, I was dismayed to think that my appearance—smiling, in broad daylight, with other people about—could cause such an emphatic recoil.

I went on down to the lake, feeling extremely angry with myself. Leaving Mr. Kurwen's eye like that on Dr. Schrever's couch had made me look like a liar and a fool. So much for my "Americanness"! And now this little incident had made me look like a dirty old man in a park.

In a rather childish fit of pique, I took Mr. Kurwen's eye from my pocket and hurled it into the half-frozen lake. Instead of landing in the water, it embedded itself in a floating island of ice, staring skyward.

Unknown to me at the time, this action was observed from the path above me, by the woman with the golden earrings.

Chapter 5

By the time our committee met on Monday, I had made up my mind what to do about Elaine.

I went up to the meeting room, Room 243, a few minutes early, in the hope of finding a moment with her alone.

She was there, but not alone. Zena Sayeed, a Palestinian mathematician, was with her. Elaine looked at me and turned away without a word. I was prepared for something like this, and had in fact made a point of wearing the same shirt—the blue one with black buttons—as a signal, should we not have an opportunity to talk until later. She looked as if she hadn't slept for the past few nights. Her eyes were red-rimmed; her face looked bloated and shapeless. Steeling myself, I went and sat next to her. She continued to ignore me. A moment later Roger arrived in the room with the fifth member of the committee.

Room 243 was a plain, drab seminar room with a chalkboard, globe lamps full of scorched moths, and a long, oak-veneer table, one side of which the five of us now occupied in a row.

As usual I took the minutes, while Roger, seated in the center, explained to us the nature of the complaint that had been brought against Bruno Jackson.

A Junior, Kenji Makota, had been grumbling about a low grade that Bruno had given him on a paper. He had told his adviser that it might have been higher if he had been "cute, with breasts." The adviser had pressed the student to explain exactly what he meant. He had then persuaded him to put his perception of Bruno's grading practices into writing.

"The point is," Roger continued, "is that if a student thinks she or he is being unfairly treated because of an instructor's involvement with *another* student, then we're obligated to start harassment proceedings, even if that other student hasn't complained. Now, under the circumstances, and Elaine will correct me if I'm wrong, I don't think we're looking at a mandatory termination of contract here, which we would be if the other student *had* complained. But we ought to at least give the guy something to think about by bringing him here in front of us. My guess is the threat of a permanent stain on his academic record ought to be enough to stop him from continuing in this pattern of behavior. That way even if he denies any involvement with his students, which he probably will given our presumption-of-guilt policy, we'll have done our job of protecting the kids, without subjecting everyone to the upheaval of a full-blown investigation. Agreed?"

We all nodded, though as I did so I cleared my throat, realizing that I had come to a decision about something that had been on my mind for several days.

"Roger," I said, "would you mind explaining the presumption-of-guilt policy?"

"It's very simple. If an instructor is discovered to be having a relationship with a student, and there's a complaint, then the presumption is he's—or she is—guilty of sexual harassment. The onus is entirely on the instructor to prove there's no harassment involved."

"By 'discovered' you mean . . ."

His blue eyes danced over my face for a moment. I felt the attention of my colleagues turn toward me, alert and curious.

"Either there's an accusation from the victim along with testimony from one or more witnesses, and the committee deems it sound, or else—"

"What about if the harassment is observed by a credible witness?"

"You mean if the harasser's caught *in flagrante*? Absolutely!"

"This is a little difficult for me," I said.

Even Elaine turned to me at this point, her reddened eyes (tear-scoured, I thought, as well as sleep-deprived) wide open. I made a point of addressing my remarks as much to her as to Roger.

"I happened to see Bruno with one of his students late the other night, down at the train station."

"A female student?" Roger asked.

"Yes."

"Was he harassing her?"

"I would have to say that he was, yes."

Zena Sayeed turned toward me.

"What was he doing?" She was a heavy-eyed, world-weary woman.

"He was trying to persuade her to go back to New York with him. He was kissing her."

"And she did not want to go with him?" Zena asked, with what I felt was an edge of private, ironic amusement.

"I heard her say that she didn't. And I had a definite sense that she wasn't comfortable being kissed. I saw her pull away from him at one point."

"What was the outcome of all this?" Roger asked.

"I don't know. My train came."

"Ah."

"How did you come to be observing them?" Zena said. "If I can ask."

I explained how I had been in the waiting room and had had no choice but to witness the scene.

"Obviously I felt very awkward about the whole thing," I added, "and to be honest, I'd made up my mind not to speak about it. One doesn't like being in the position of a tattletale. But I think that on balance not to say anything would have been the cowardly thing to do. Either we take our responsibility here seriously, or else we might as well pack up and go home."

Roger nodded vigorously. "I agree with you a hundred percent. This is courageous of you, Lawrence. The question is, what happens now? Elaine, suggestion?"

I hadn't known whether I would come out with all this until I actually began speaking, but I had certainly formed the opinion that it was the right thing to do. Despite the superficial associations with spying and informing, it seemed to me that to tell what I knew would be consistent with the straightforward, "plain-dealing" approach to life I aspired to. And in fact I had found it pleasantly liberating to speak so openly. It gave me a feeling of robustness and courage—so much so that I felt bold enough to begin implementing, right there and then, my other big decision of the day; the one concerning Elaine.

As she paused for thought before answering Roger, I placed my hand on her thigh, under the table. This had an electrifying effect. She sat up with a jolt as if she'd been bitten, but then immediately disguised the action as a violent coughing spasm.

"Excuse me," she managed after a moment, patting her chest.

"Can I get you a drink of water?" Roger asked.

"No, no, I'm fine. Sorry."

Far from trying to remove my hand, Elaine placed her own hand surreptitiously over it as soon as she had recovered herself sufficiently to do so.

"To answer your question, Roger," she said, "I think it would be appropriate to add what Lawrence has told us to the documentation concerning Bruno. As far as termination of contract, it probably would need to be supported by a complaint from the student in question. But in the meantime it adds to the pressure on this instructor to leave these kids alone."

"You think we should tell him we know about this involvement?"

Elaine looked at me. She spoke neutrally, but her tired eyes were shining again.

"That would be up to Lawrence, I guess."

I squeezed her thigh tenderly. Her lip gave a discreet quiver.

"He knows I saw him," I said.

"So then he may as well know you've told us," Roger put in, "unless you strongly object, Lawrence?"

"It's not something I relish. But if there's no other way around it . . ."

Roger looked pensive for a moment.

"Perhaps on second thought we'll keep this to ourselves," he said, "until the student herself complains. You don't happen to know who she was?"

"Candida something?"

Zena Sayeed raised a dark eyebrow at this: "Candy Johanssen? Skinny girl? Sort of a Pre-Raphaelite starveling?"

"That sounds like her."

"She's my advisee."

Roger turned to her. "Then perhaps you might want to have a word with her, Zena."

Zena made a noncommittal sound.

"Do you have a problem with that?" Roger asked; not aggressively, but with a surprising forcefulness that impressed me again with the strength of his passion in this cause. Apparently he was prepared to ruffle a few feathers to get the results he wanted.

Zena eyed him a moment—debating, I sensed, whether it was worth getting into a discussion.

"Not at all," she said pleasantly. "I'll speak to her."

Roger pressed his advantage: "It sounds to me as though there may be a psychological endangerment issue here. You say she's thin?"

"As a rail."

"I think you should speak to her, Zena."

"I said I would, and I will."

A few minutes later Bruno was brought into the room by the dean's assistant.

One would have thought that with the threat of the ultimate stigma of his profession hanging over his head, he might have appeared nervous, but it was evident at once that he had decided to adopt a posture of casual indifference toward the proceedings.

He gave us an affable sort of a grin and sat sideways in his chair, sprawling an arm over the back.

He looked at me. "Hello, Lawrence," he said quietly.

I felt again the pressure of his peculiar and unrequited urge to make an accomplice of me. I nodded at him, glad that I had made my feelings about him clear to my colleagues, though uncomfortable at the appearance of duplicitousness that his friendly attitude seemed calculated to promote.

"So. What atrocity have I committed?"

Refusing to rise to the bait of Bruno's scorn, Roger proceeded to explain the charge of unfair grading, and how, under the cir-

cumstances, this had opened Bruno to the graver charge of sexual harassment.

"I've never harassed anyone in my life," Bruno interrupted in
his rasping voice. "Personally, I've never needed to."

"And we're anxious," Roger put in gently, "that you don't find
yourself accused of it. Which is why we asked you to come and
meet with us."

"Who's threatening to accuse me of it?"

"Bruno, if I may, two things. . . ." Roger spoke in his calm, dis-
passionate way. "Number one, since we don't, unlike some other
colleges, have a rule saying you absolutely can't get involved with
students, the onus is on us to keep the barrier of protection especially high. You can make the choice to have an affair with a student, but at your own risk. The first whisper of a complaint from
the student, you're presumed guilty of harassment and you're
out of here, period."

"Has there been a whisper?"

"No. Not yet. Not from a student. But my second point, Bruno,
is that you have a rich and rewarding career ahead of you.
You're on tenure track here, you're clearly a gifted teacher, why
blow it?"

"No whisper of harassment from a student, but a whisper
from someone else?"

"That—that's not something you have to trouble yourself with
for the moment."

"Then what are you driving at, Roger?"

"At this point I think if you would give us an undertaking not
to go any further along this road than you may have already
gone, that ought to be sufficient. Yes?" Roger looked at each of
us. We nodded, and he turned back to Bruno.

Bruno merely gave a disdainful grin. "I'll take my chances
with the whisperers," he replied swaggeringly. I felt that his eyes

were upon me, though I had my own firmly down on the page of minutes before me.

"Am I free to go now?" he asked.

Roger sighed. "Yes. But please keep in mind that we're charged with certain responsibilities here, and that we do take them seriously."

Bruno stood up. "I'll keep it in mind."

There was a silence after the door closed.

"So much for that," Roger said quietly. "Zena, you'll have a word with your student?"

"I'll do what I can, Roger," Zena replied wearily. Even she seemed to have been disturbed by Bruno's attitude.

A few minutes later I was walking across campus with Elaine by my side. The afternoon had turned soft and sunny. Over the distant roar of traffic, you could hear the trickle of melted snow running into the storm drains. For a while we moved together in silence—a silence that I sensed was highly charged for her.

"I'd almost given up on you," she said at last, her voice thick.

"I'm sorry." I didn't attempt to explain why I hadn't been in touch.

"Oh, no, *I'm* sorry. I was just so—excited, I guess."

"That's good. I want you to feel excited."

"Oh . . . thank you for saying that."

"What would you like to do?" I asked.

"I'd like to cook you a meal. That's what I'd like to do."

"I was hoping you might say that."

"I'm famous for my cauliflower quiche."

"My mouth's watering already."

"Oh, you!" she said, laughing. She scribbled the directions to her house on a scrap of paper, and we parted with a fond, liquid look into each other's eyes.

Since she lived near the next train station up along the line, it wasn't worth my while going back into Manhattan before dinner. I had two hours to kill. I went to my office, picking up a yellow interdepartmental envelope from my mailbox on the way. Inside was the piece Amber had asked me to look at. Reluctantly, I laid it on my desk and began to read, but I found myself completely unable to concentrate on it. I was thinking of its author—the way she seemed to suspend herself so vividly in the inner proscenium of my consciousness whenever I was in her presence, and the apprehension this always aroused.

At once I caught a trace of something from the distant past: a faint resonance, like the last, almost inaudible reverberation of a gong.

It sometimes seems to me that the mind—my own, at least— far from being the infinitely capacious organ one likes to think it is, is in fact rather rudimentary, possessing only a very limited number of categories for the things it experiences, and lumping all kinds of diverse phenomena together on the basis of the most accidental resemblance. That would account for the way you realize from time to time that you have never made a real distinction between, say, the dog-owning neighbor in the town you were born in, and the cat-owning neighbor in the town you moved to later on. Both have simply been categorized as "pet-owning neighbors." It's always a bit of a shock when you realize that the people or things you've fused together have nothing to do with each other at all.

In the case of Amber, what I realized was that I had combined her image with that of a figure from my adolescence: Emily Lloyd, my stepfather's daughter.

It wasn't that they looked like each other. Emily had thick chestnut ringlets; she was petite, with a watchful, smoothly angular face, while Amber was long-limbed, willowy, even a little gawky; a bit like a giraffe foal, in fact, with her freckles and short red-gold hair.

But the feeling each aroused in me was the same: a desire so sharp (I had had to acknowledge that Amber's effect on me amounted to this) it seemed more to do with recovering something vital and precious that had been taken from me than with gaining possession of something new. That, and a feeling of confronting something capable of destroying me.

Not wishing to think about either of them, I scanned the bookshelves for something to distract me.

A small collected Shakespeare caught my eye. I took it down and opened the front cover. In faded green ink, the handwriting as neat as a row of pines on a mountain ridge, was the following inscription:

To our beloved Barbara,
A gift to remind you how much we treasure you as you go off to
college and embark on your life's great dream.
Your ever-loving Mom and Dad
September 8th 1985

The late Barbara Hellermann, I presumed: Trumilcik's successor in this room, and my own immediate predecessor; brewer of coffee for her students, recipient of thank-you notes, collector of uplifting quotations . . . and quite a bit younger, judging from the date she went off to college, than I had imagined. Not more than her mid-thirties, it would seem, when she died: a painful thought, especially in the context of the parents' loving inscription. With a small internal rustle—a little inner scene-shifting—

the kind-old-lady image I had formed of her was replaced by that of a young woman in the tragic flush of some rare illness. Poignant, though since I had no personal connection, only superficially distressing.

Leafing through the silky pages of the volume, I came to *Measure for Measure*. I hadn't looked at the play since my teens, but the lines were as familiar to me as if I had written them myself. There was the sexual miscreant Claudio, that "warpèd slip of wilderness," on death row for his sins. There was his judge, Angelo, "this ungenitured agent," as the dissolute scoffer Lucio calls him, battling (with underappreciated sincerity, I felt) his own ungovernable urges. And there was Claudio's sister, chaste Isabella, about to enter the cloisters when she encounters Angelo, triggering his explosive lust. I took her part once in our all-boys "O" Level class, and I recalled now the queasy excitement it had given me to announce that I would rather die than accept Angelo's offer to spare my brother's life if I would sleep with him. *Were I under terms of death,* I remembered declaiming passionately, *th'impression of keen whips I'd wear as rubies. . . .*

I took the volume over to my desk, meaning to reread the play. I hadn't got far, though, when Emily Lloyd started drifting back into my thoughts. It occurred to me that I must have come into contact with her right around the time we were studying this play. I was fifteen, home from school, where my stepfather was now paying the fees. I remember him tousling my hair as I arrived at the little station near the weekend cottage he'd bought my mother in Kent. I put down my bags and we shared a look of helplessness. We were less than nothing to each other—a void; the shape of an absence. In his case his own children; in mine, my father, who'd died of a brain tumor when I was five.

The house was tiny; all that Robert—my stepfather—had been able to afford now that his ex-wife had his finances tied up. It was a former plowman's cottage, with minute windows. My mother filled the little rooms with rustic bric-a-brac, but it remained obstinately gloomy, and every time the three of us spent any time there together, the effort of not getting on each other's nerves would distill itself into a fine, potent melancholy that tended to engulf us in silence after a few hours.

"You look a bit peaky, dear," my mother said to me that evening.

"I'm fine."

"You're not bored, are you?"

"No."

"I think it's a dreadful shame you didn't want to bring one of your friends to stay."

"I'm all right."

"There's lots to do. Bike rides, sailing on the reservoir. . . . I should have thought they'd jump at the opportunity to come and stay."

"I'm supposed to be revising."

I couldn't tell her it was out of the question that I should ever bring a friend here. There was an absolute veto on the subject in my mind. The form it took was a sense that everything that occurred in our household was blighted with a deep wrongness of spirit. I didn't know where this sense had originated, but I knew it was so. Under our roof, the simplest observation on the weather was liable to sound insincere or manipulative; the social functions my mother liked to arrange had a fraught, overelaborate quality that made everyone long for them to be over. With the resignation one learns at the kind of schools I went to, I accepted all this as my lot in life, but I had no wish to share it with anyone else.

Even so, my mother was right: I was bored, and I was lonely.

"It's a pity the Bestridges don't seem to want to know us,"

she pressed on. "They have a boy Lawrence's age don't they, Robert?"

"Do they?"

My stepfather was ensconced behind his newspaper with a glass of white port, his long legs in their well-cut pinstripes sprawling with an incongruous languor toward the diminutive fireplace.

"Why don't you invite them over for cocktails?"

He lowered his newspaper, glancing at her through the tops of his bifocals.

"We've been through that, dear."

"Have we? Well, I think it's very silly that we can't invite them for cocktails just because they haven't had time to invite us back for dinner yet. I think it's very stuffy and conventional, if you must know."

"If they'd wanted to socialize with us, they'd have found time to invite us over in the year and a half since we had them to dinner, don't you think?"

"How would I know? I'm not them. Anyway, why wouldn't they want to socialize with us?"

"I can't imagine."

"It isn't as if they have any right to be high and mighty with us. You're a company director. Lawrence goes to a perfectly good school. I may be a bit of a nobody, but at least I'm not a frump, which can't exactly be said of Jill Bestridge. I should have thought they'd want to bend over backwards to be friends with us. Perhaps they're shy, perhaps that's all it is, Robert. Perhaps they need more encouragement. Robert?"

"Perhaps."

"Oh, you're no help!"

"You can't force people to like you, Geraldine, dear. It's against the laws of physics."

He turned the page of his newspaper and shook it straight with a single practiced snap.

My mother stood up and wandered about the room, fussing with her ornaments and flowers. She wasn't done with this topic, I could tell. Her restless, aggrieved spirit never settled easily, once aroused.

I sensed also that she hadn't yet come to her point, her *real* point; that to get to it she had to conjure a more vexed and petulant atmosphere than currently prevailed.

"I don't see how you ever get what you want in life if you aren't prepared to push a little. You have to push! I've had to push people all *my* life."

"And you wonder why people find you pushy."

"Do they?" My mother asked, her violet-blue eyes suddenly wide and vulnerable.

I could see that my stepfather regretted his riposte.

"No, dear, I'm just saying they *would*—"

"Is that why the Bestridges don't—"

"Don't let's start, Geraldine—"

"I suppose you think I pushed *you*. Is that what you think?"

"Geraldine—"

"All those afternoon drinkies at the Portingham Cellars—was that me pushing you? Those romantic tête-à-têtes down in the storage room at Findley Street, did I push you down there? Did I? Pushy Geraldine shoving poor weak Mr. Robert Julius Lloyd down the basement stairs in the middle of the morning when she couldn't wait another second for a bit of what you fancy, is that how you remember it, darling?"

My stepfather sighed, folding away his newspaper. He disliked confrontations, and would agree to almost any demand in order to avoid them. His own dissatisfactions he worked out silently and in private, in stratagems that didn't emerge until their fruit was already fully ripened. For all I know, as he sat there gazing mildly at my mother, he was already plotting how to start siphoning off funds to set up the flat (or "love nest," as the newspapers later called it) for his new mistress, a private casino waitress by the name of Brandy Colquhoun, whose existence burst on us a year or so later.

"What is it you want, my love?"

"Want? I don't *want* anything. I'd *like* to think I had a husband who took some interest in the well-being of my child—"

"Geraldine, I'm simply saying I don't think the Bestridges—"

"Oh who cares about the Bestridges? Do you think I care tuppence about those snobs?"

"Well what is it you want me to do?"

"What's the point of even discussing what I want you to do, since you refuse to do anything I suggest anyway?"

"What have I ever refused?"

My mother looked away from him; adjusted a dried rose.

In a quiet voice, she said:

"The Royal Aldersbury, for one thing."

There.

"Ah, now, Geraldine . . ."

"What? Just because your daughter's a member, does that mean it's too good for Lawrence? I find that a little bit insulting, if you must know."

The Royal Aldersbury was a sports club for well-to-do county families. Robert's daughter Emily was a member and, from what I could gather, spent all her free time there, in a gilded haze of tennis tournaments, dinghy regattas, and country dances.

It was near the Lloyd house, twelve miles from us, on the banks of a wide stretch of the Medway. Robert met his daughter and two young sons there for tea every Sunday, an event from which he would return in a state of dejection that my mother had come to feel offended by, so that they had had to institute a counterritual of dining out at an expensive restaurant—the White Castle or the Gay Hussar—every Sunday night when they arrived back in London.

Several times she had raised the subject of Robert getting me into the Royal Aldersbury, ostensibly so that I would have something to do when I came to the cottage, though the more Robert had resisted the idea, the more firmly it had acquired the higher significance of a measure of his current regard for her. Robert was too much of the English school of obtuseness to say right out that he was afraid it might upset his daughter to have to mix with the son of the woman he'd left his family for, but that was evidently what he felt, and my mother found this mortifying. She had taken the position that once she and Robert had married, the entire situation regarding both families had become irrevocably normalized and stable, almost to the point of retroactively annulling the fact of his previous marriage. She often tried to get Robert to bring his children to our home, and even hinted that it was about time he took us over to visit his former wife. Perhaps she had visions of joining Selena Lloyd and her set for ladies' luncheons in Tunbridge Wells.

Even so, she was probably as surprised as I was when Robert suddenly stood up and telephoned the Royal Aldersbury, asking to speak to the club secretary.

A few minutes later I was a probationary member.

"Satisfied?" he asked my mother, sitting back down to his newspaper. He was affecting nonchalance, but he must have been aware of the magnitude of what he had done; its fundamental destructiveness. I suspect he was the type of man who even took a certain fastidious pleasure in setting off small avalanches of this nature: proving to himself and the world just how much of a source of disorder he was.

My mother was pleased: deeply, physically pleased. She flushed, and her eyes shone. She brought the bottle of white port over to Robert and filled his glass. They were guarded about showing physical affection in front of me, but they had evolved numerous small acts of attention that by now were as obvious an indication of the flow of feeling between them as the deepest of French kisses would have been.

The next morning my stepfather took me to the Royal Aldersbury. It was a fine spring day: the May was flowering in the hedges and the apple orchards were in bloom. We drove in silence: by tacit agreement we never spoke to each other when my mother wasn't around.

The main building of the club was a grand, gabled, chimneyed pile covered in Virginia creeper. Around it were tennis courts, squash courts, croquet lawns, a badminton lawn with stout-legged ladies leaping around in pleated tutus; and at the back, gliding blackly in its flower-filled banks, the river.

Robert took me uptairs to meet the treasurer and secretary. He was politely aloof with these functionaries, who appeared to regard him as a mighty personage. An enigmatic smile played across his features as they made conversation with him, supplying their own answers when none was forthcoming from him. Though I had no idea what he was thinking, I felt that he was privately amusing himself at everyone else's expense. I didn't mind.

A woman came to the door and signaled to the treasurer. He tiptoed over to her, murmuring an apology. They stood in the next room talking in hushed voices, then the treasurer tiptoed back. He cleared his throat:

"It would appear that Mrs. Lloyd is taking tea in the main

lobby with Miss Lloyd. Would you—would you like us to take you out through the side door Mr. Lloyd . . . ah . . . discreet . . ."

"No. I was hoping she'd be here. I want to introduce Lawrence."

The treasurer and secretary looked nervously at him. Though they probably didn't expect anything so vulgar as a "scene" to occur, they were the kind of creatures to whom a situation with even the potential for a scene, even where that potential is sure to remain firmly suppressed, is a source of anxiety.

After I had filled out my forms and signed the membership book—an ancient volume with a column in it for your title as well as your name and address—I followed Robert back down to the main lobby, which was now alive with the particular muted but purposeful buzz of the upper classes going about their leisure.

Mrs. Lloyd and her daughter were seated in an alcove half-screened by potted palms. As we approached them, I saw at once that the daughter was beautiful, and moreover beautiful in a way that so intimately corresponded to my ideal conception of female beauty at the time, that it was hard to resist the feeling that she had been created and placed there expressly for my personal delectation. My interest in the place, till then not nearly as strong as my mother's, abruptly sharpened.

Mrs. Lloyd, a smaller, sallower, skinnier woman than I had imagined, gave a brief start as she saw us, but quickly recovered her composure. Emily looked gravely at her father, her bee-stung little mouth firmly closed.

"I want you to meet Lawrence," Robert said. The same aloof, secretive smile played on his face. Perhaps it was just his way of showing embarrassment, though its effect was to suggest he wasn't actually present in the situation at all, other than in the most banally literal way.

"Geraldine's son," he added.

Mother and daughter looked at me blank-faced.

"Pleased to meet you," I said, immediately noticing a look flash between all three Lloyds.

"Emily, I was hoping you might show Lawrence around. Introduce him to your friends. He doesn't know anyone here. Would you do that?"

The girl seemed stunned, almost benumbed, by the situation. But she said yes with an obedient simplicity as though it would never have crossed her mind to oppose her father's will.

"Good. Well, then. I'll see you on Sunday, dear. Lawrence, I'll pick you up at six."

To his ex-wife he merely nodded, receiving the faintest of nods in return.

Emily was true to her word. After her mother left, which she did as soon as was civilly possible, she gave me a tour of the building and grounds, introducing me to various teenage acquaintances on the way. She made no attempt to converse with me, and was largely unresponsive to my remarks. Even so, I felt that I was making a favorable impression on her. I was intensely smitten by her. The thick, reddish brown spill of her ringlets, her agate eyes, her sharply chiseled nose and pointed, elfin chin, were altogether too close to my image of that longed-for but hitherto entirely elusive entity, a *girlfriend*, for me to be capable of separating her from my fantasy. Her prolonged presence by my side as we strolled through the club began to acquire a meaning of its own in my imagination; something more than just duty and circumstance could account for. In some ineffable way we were "together"—a fact that seemed further cemented every time she introduced me to someone new. Her voice was soft and clear, with a faint, nascent edge of imperiousness. She wore a perfume that rapidly insinuated itself into the deepest cortical centers of my brain: even today, when I catch it in a store or lobby, I am instantly back in her sweetly enchanting aura.

By the time we finished our tour, I was feeling distinctly proprietorial about her. Doubtless she expected me to wander off by myself now, but the thought didn't even cross my mind, and she was too well brought up to say anything.

Some friends of hers came up, and as I persisted in lingering by her, she introduced me to them. These, it turned out, were her particular set, and over the next three days I got to know them well. The mere fact of Emily's introducing me appeared to be enough to gain their acceptance. No doubt she found a way of quietly explaining who I was, but she must not have conveyed any particular antipathy on that score, because they included me in all their activities as if it were the most natural thing in the world.

Like her, they were extremely polite and superbly confident. The boys were constantly standing up and offering their seats to older women. The girls—Fiona, Rosamond, Sophia, Lucy—were miracles of deportment and elocution, their adolescent bodies always under perfect control. Their facial expressions had the sophistication of seasoned matrons—little nuances of irony, *moues* of mock petulance, casting a wonderful allure over the most neutral of remarks. But nothing off-color or spiteful was ever intimated. They seemed almost conscious of a responsibility to set an example of gracious conduct, whether they were lobbing an easy ball to a weaker player over the tennis net, or complimenting the dinner ladies on the rhubarb pie in the dining room.

Among the boys was one I immediately identified as a rival. His name was Justin Brady. He was good-looking—tall, with a supple athletic build, wavy black hair, and a cheerful, animated face. There was some kind of understanding between him and Emily. At first I thought he might actually be her boyfriend, but they never held hands or kissed, as some of the others did, so I ruled that out. But when we first played doubles he seemed to take it for granted that he would partner Emily, and later, when she mentioned that she wouldn't mind going out on the river for a sail, he seemed to assume this meant she wanted him to go with her.

In both instances I managed to ward him off by sheer force of will. I simply stuck by her at her end of the court, creating a standoff until, with a pleasant grin, Justin retreated to the other end. And when it was decided that we should all go sailing, I pre-empted him by asking Emily outright if she would come in my dinghy. She did hesitate a moment, looking at Justin, but he merely gave his pleasant warm smile again and told her to go ahead.

Out on the river a mild breeze, scented with the flowers that grew on the banks, puffed out our sails and sent us rippling across the water. Emily said nothing, barely looked at me, but I felt that I was in paradise. To the extent that I even noticed her unresponsiveness, I put it down to shyness and her generally subdued manner. This was almost enough; almost all I wanted of love at that moment, to be gliding silently across the river with this bewitching girl. My own sails were filled! There had been talk of the upcoming Easter Dance, some preliminary discussion of partners and costumes. It seemed to me an inevitability that Emily would come as my partner; that we would dance all evening, and seal our budding romance with a long, tender kiss out on a balcony.

By the second day I had half-intoxicated myself with the imagined taste of her kisses, the sensation of plying my hands through her wondrous mass of ringlets. I spent the day waiting for opportunities to gaze into her eyes. On the rare occasions when she looked back at me, it was with a curious, dazed expression, as though we were meeting in a dream.

The next day her mother had to pick her up earlier than usual.
On the spur of the moment, a general invitation to tea was
issued. It didn't cross my mind that I might not be welcome at
Robert's former home, and I ran to get my things along with the
rest of them. When I turned up at her Land Rover, Mrs. Lloyd
frowned slightly. Wasn't Robert expecting to pick me up at the
club later that afternoon? she asked. Gently, with the effusive
politeness I had learned from my new friends, I assured her she
needn't worry—I would ring him from her house and he could
pick me up there instead. Since she appeared to operate at a
fairly cool temperature at the best of times, I didn't think anything of the frostiness with which she received this, and I piled
into the car next to Emily.

The home was a dilapidated Elizabethan manor. Dwarf apple
trees stood blossoming through lichenous old limbs in a garden
enclosed by a crumbling brick wall. Inside, fragrances such as
only the action of long centuries can distill out of worn stone,
polished elm, dust, silver, and old glass, hung in the tall rooms. I
wandered through with a sense of having gained admittance to
some inner precinct of existence, where every sensation was rar-
efied to an almost melancholy sweetness and purity. My spirit
seemed to open here. I felt that I was converging with some
design deeply inscribed in my own destiny; one that had been
guiding me toward this place for many years without my knowing it, and that intended to connect me to it with the strongest,
most intimate bonds.

We had tea in the drawing room. Emily's younger brothers
joined us. They stared at me, not saying a word. I didn't mind:
there was all the time in the world, I felt, to befriend them. Mrs.
Lloyd kept coming in with cakes and sandwiches. We boys stood
up for her every time she entered, pressing her to sit down and
join us, but she wouldn't.

After tea we trooped up to Emily's bedroom to listen to records on her new stereo. Her bed was an old four-poster with a carved wooden canopy. I felt a kindliness emanate from it; a sense that it and I were going to become old friends.

We sat around on cushions, chatting, laughing, listening to music. I couldn't help feeling that it was for me in particular that this event had been orchestrated. I smiled indulgently at the others, interred so blissfully in my own folly that I half-expected them to start leaving one by one so that Emily and I could finally be alone.

Justin took charge of the stereo without being invited to. I tried not to let this interfere with my expansive mood, but after a while it started to bother me. I felt uncomfortable more on Emily's behalf than my own. I stood up and, with what I thought was a friendly but firm decisiveness, changed the record he had just put on and stationed myself by the controls. With his usual good grace, Justin backed off at once. I noticed a few looks being exchanged among the others, but I felt that all they signified was a growing acknowledgment of the intimacy developing between Emily and myself.

The beat of the music went through us, binding us together as we nodded our heads in time, or sang along with snatches of the melody. I felt the surging happiness you only ever experience at that age—the euphoria of being part of a group of friends traveling together into the future. Love overflows your heart; you feel an almost religious joy, as though some divine emissary had alighted right there in the midst of your little congregation.

Emily was quiet, but the rest of us were animated—talking about our lives, our schools, our families. The subject of mothers came up. Fiona's mother was a Tory councillor. The mother of one of the boys raised some rare breed of sheep. "What about your mother, Lawrence?" somebody asked me. "What does she do?" I was just thinking how best to answer when Emily spoke, her voice quiet but clear as a bell above the music:

"She's sort of a high-class prostitute, isn't she?"

What I felt at first was simply a loss of bearings, as though some natural disaster had just occurred. The euphoria was still inside me, still surging on its own momentum, and in the hush that followed Emily's remark, I heard myself blurt with what I thought was tremendous quick-wittedness, "actually, no, she's a *low*-class prostitute," whereupon a strange ballooning lightness seemed to raise me up to my feet and carry me involuntarily out of the room and downstairs, where Mrs. Lloyd informed me that Robert was on his way to pick me up, and that I would be doing her a great kindness if I would leave immediately and wait for him at the end of the driveway so that he wouldn't have to come to the house.

As I stumbled off, the magnitude and horror of what had just occurred—what had been occurring, I grasped dimly, throughout the past three days—broke on me in little astounding illuminations. It was more than I could absorb all at once. Little dazzling glimpses of it burst inside me. The effect was largely physical. I didn't know whether I wanted to sob or throw up.

I've had my share of snubs and insults since then, but nothing has ever had such a decisive effect on me. My own part in it dismayed me more than anything else. For years afterward I could make myself writhe in undiminished pain at the thought of my obnoxious behavior during those three days. How clearly I could see in hindsight the growing hatred I was arousing in Emily's friends as I strutted about among them. Yet how sure I had been of their love at the time!

Was it really possible to be so catastrophically wrong in one's reading of a situation? The discovery that it was disturbed me profoundly. I have distrusted myself ever since. Anytime I begin to feel comfortable with people, I immediately conjecture a parallel version of myself arousing their secret loathing. Pretty soon it gets hard to tell which version reflects reality, and I find myself splitting the difference; withdrawing into an attitude of detached neutrality.

I sat there in Room 106 remembering these things. I hadn't dredged them up for years, but every detail was as fresh and vivid in my memory as ever. A plausible hell, I have often thought, could be made out of such incidents, relived *ad infinitum*.

While going over them, I had swiveled my chair around and put my feet up on the shelf behind my desk, so that I was in a reclining position. Lying that way, I was in the same relation to Trumilcik's lair as I was to Dr. Schrever's chair when I lay in her office. Had I in some way been substituting Trumilcik for Dr. Schrever as I relived these moments? Perhaps I thought that as a European he might understand better than she the structure of inhibitions and concealed hierarchies that made such an event possible. At any rate, by the time I was finished, I felt the pleasantly calm, spent sensation I sometimes felt at the end of my sessions with Dr. Schrever.

With that in mind, I took a couple of twenty-dollar bills from my wallet and left them on the desk by Amber's pages: an offering for Trumilcik, should he come tonight. I had formed the idea that he was living pretty much hand to mouth, and I felt I owed him something for co-opting his spirit as a stand-in for Dr. Schrever. I also wanted to demonstrate to him my good will; my solidarity with him as an ex-pat from the Old World trying to plant his feet in the New.

Then I set off for Elaine's.

Chapter 6

It was getting dark. Treetops made shatter-line patterns against the glassy strip of horizon. I was in a state of deliberate suspension: suspended judgment, suspended feeling. I was following a plan of my own devising, but passively, in a state of deliberately suspended will.

In a women's clothing store on Mulberry Street, I saw a V-neck sweater of gray wool with flower-embroidered cuffs. It was exactly the kind of thing Carol wore: austere, with an impishly begrudged femininity. I'd have bought it for her without hesitating if we'd still been living together. I did things like that, and she seemed to appreciate them. I was beginning to move reluctantly away when I decided to buy the sweater anyway. It was expensive, but just having it in my possession seemed to bring me a step closer to some hypothetical moment in the future when I would have the opportunity to give it to her.

Strange, at the station, to move off in the opposite direction from usual. Out in the twilight a row of shacks went by. Zigzagging white Christmas lights—a new type that had taken over the country like an invasive weed—fringed the plastic-roofed decks. Beyond them was an old assembly plant with a row of truck cabins—just the cabins—moldering in front of it like gigantic skulls in some dinosaur graveyard. Then, after that, stranger still in the dregs of the daylight, a ghostly fairground, abandoned decades ago, by the look of it; the blown husks and bracts of some bygone era's little flowering of fun. A radial of horseless spokes was all that survived of the merry-go-round. Over a small wooden booth I made out the capital H and M of two otherwise illegible words in faded circus lettering. Whatever came next the scrub had knitted a snarl of creepers over, obliterating all but a few dark forms that looked like ruins in a jungle.

Elaine's station was a lonely strip of platform in a near-empty parking lot. As I got in a taxi, I discovered I had left the scrap of paper with her directions on it behind, presumably in my office. Oddly enough, given my recent forgetfulness, I remembered the address without difficulty, even though I had only looked at it once, as she wrote it down. I took this to be a good omen.

The town was just a series of new residential developments: twenty or thirty identical houses in each, with identical blobs of shrubbery out front and big signs offering units for sale. I had seen these kinds of places on summer days. The people you saw drifting around them wore pajama-like clothes, as though their conception of leisure was inextricably bound up with the idea of sleep. Lincoln Court, where Elaine lived, was still partly under construction. Plywood-covered frames stuck up out of the raw dirt, and between some of the houses there were still patches of old, scrubby farmland, not yet reprocessed into manicured lawns. The cold air smelled of pressure-treated lumber. I paid the taxi and went up the short path to Elaine's door.

Perfume billowed up at me as she opened it. There she was, a look of ardent joy spilling from her eyes. She wore a lemon-colored chemise and a brown, calf-length, hip-hugging skirt.

Before arriving, I had made up my mind that I would greet her with a light kiss on the lips. For a moment now I balked: there was something softly overpowering about her; her indefinite features rendered somehow daunting by the formalized glamour of her outfit. I braced myself, however, plunged my head into the cloud of scent, and brushed my lips against hers. She seemed surprised by the gesture, but not displeased. She led me into a gray-carpeted room with prints of semi-abstract flowers on the wall. At the back was a tile-floored dining area with a glass table set for two.

The place felt brand-new: unpenetrated yet by its human inhabitant.

I sat on a denim-covered couch, oatmeal in color, while Elaine poured me a drink. It crossed my mind that I should have brought something—flowers, or at least a bottle of wine.

Handing me my drink, Elaine looked hesitantly at the space next to me on the couch. I patted it, and she lowered the sweetened weight of herself into the cushion beside me. I took her hand and gave it a squeeze.

"I'm so glad you could come," she said.

I had given up trying to figure out what it was I could have said or done to bring this situation into being. I accepted it in all its strangeness: looked on it as a premise rather than a result. The question in my mind was where to go from here.

I hadn't slept with a woman for some time—long enough that my thoughts and dreams had started decomposing into erotic fantasies with a frequency I hadn't experienced in years. Theoretically the idea of leveraging my apparently substantial credit with Elaine into some kind of fling had a certain appeal; or would have, if I had felt the slightest physical attraction to her, which so far I had not.

But that indifference, related as it was to a similarly unqualified emotional indifference, was possibly not the end of the story. Whenever I had denied to Dr. Schrever that I was attracted to her, or missed her between sessions, or had tried to hurt her by not showing up, she would suggest that I wasn't necessarily able to experience the reality of my own feelings. I had always privately dismissed this as an example of the kind of cant her profession was prone to, but in view of some of the things that had been happening recently, I had begun to wonder if there mightn't really be some kind of interference between the feelings I had and my ability to register them.

Was it possible, I had wondered, that I was attracted to Elaine without knowing it? Such a thing seemed beyond the bounds of likelihood, but I found I couldn't dismiss it out of hand. My unconscious choice of her name for the mistress in *S for Salmon* was surely an indication of something. Perhaps if I placed myself in her presence for long enough, I had thought, my feelings might become sufficiently focused to make themselves known to me.

Was that why I had come here tonight? Partly. But I was aware of something else too: something obscurely, soothingly expiatory in deferring to another person's version of reality. As if there were something significant to be gained by giving myself to this woman out of nothing more than sheer self-sacrificing agreeableness.

I turned to her. She looked at me expectantly. I felt her vulnerability; her strange humility too, and under it the throb of a real passion: incomprehensible to me, but undeniable.

"I brought you something," I heard myself say, standing up.

With a vague feeling of annoyance, I realized I was going to take the bag with Carol's sweater in it from my briefcase and give it to Elaine. I did this.

She unwrapped it. "You got me a sweater!" She said, beaming. "Thank you, Lawrence. Thanks so much!"

She held it up against her chest.

"That's just so gorgeous! I'm so flattered you would think to do a thing like that!"

"Why don't you try it on?"

"I will. But not over this. Wait right there."

She went out of the room. I heard her go upstairs. A moment later, I wandered up myself.

"Can I see up here?" I called out.

"Help yourself."

There was a spare room with a single bed on a gray fitted carpet; bare walls. The bathroom next to it was green tile and chrome; spotless, with fluffy green towels neatly folded over the rack. I knocked on the bedroom door.

"Oh . . . come in."

This also was strangely featureless, like a hotel room: the bed immaculately flat and smooth under its gold-brown bedspread; the bedside table with its brass reading lamp, china tissue dispenser, red-digit radio-alarm. A black TV faced it from the dresser opposite. There was an infant's wooden rocker with a rag doll asprawl in it, but even that seemed like something that might have been supplied along with the rest of the fixtures. The only noticeably personal touch was a small, hand-painted wooden box on the dressing table. Otherwise the aspiration here seemed to be toward total anonymity.

Elaine stepped out from behind the opened closet door, smoothing the sweater down over her front.

"What do you think?"

It was tight on her: she must have been a couple of sizes larger than Carol. But the sight of her in it had an immediate effect on me. I saw there were possibilities in this situation that I hadn't considered. It wasn't that she resembled my wife, but she put me in mind of her, and the very lack of any powerful singularity about herself or her home allowed the thought to grow more vivid.

"You look spectacular," I told her.

She coughed and reddened, patting her chest.

"Thank you!"

I was struck again by the curious dominion her version of me seemed to possess over her. In deferring to her sense of what existed between us, I appeared to have put myself in a position of paradoxical power.

I took her hands in mine and drew her close, smiling at her. She smiled back. Then with a playful laugh she freed one of her hands and placed it on the little painted box.

"Guess what I keep in here."

"What?"

"Guess!"

"Your husband?"

She gave a peal of laughter. "You are so funny!"

"What, then?"

"What would be the most precious thing I could have in my possession, other than yourself?"

"I can't imagine."

"Oh, Lawrence! Your *letter*, of course!"

I had never written her a letter. I must have looked disconcerted.

"Did I say something wrong?" she asked.

I felt instinctively that I should try to conceal my puzzlement, at least until I had figured out what was going on.

"Not at all," I managed. "I'm—I guess I'm just—moved."

A look of joy blazed from her eyes.

"Let's eat."

As if the mystery of this letter were not enough to keep me thoroughly distracted for the rest of the evening, something even more disturbing arose soon after. As I passed my open briefcase on my way into the dining room, I happened to glimpse Barbara Hellermann's volume of Shakespeare, which I had brought to read on the train home.

"Incidentally," I said, "did you know Barbara Hellermann?"

She looked blank for a moment.

"Oh, Lord—you mean the woman who got killed?"

"She was killed?"

"You didn't know?"

"No." With an obscure apprehensiveness, I asked what had happened.

"Some crazy guy in the subway attacked her. She went into a coma, then died just a few days later. I knew her to say hello, but—"

"Did they catch the guy?"

"I don't believe they did."

"How did he—how did he kill her?"

"He hit her with a steel bar."

Over the cauliflower quiche I tried to maintain the appearance of a besotted admirer, asking Elaine about her life and nodding interestedly as she told me about it, but my mind was elsewhere. I was preoccupied with the question of how soon I could decently leave, and whether there would be time to stop off at my office before the last train home. The result was that I took in only snatches of what she was saying to me, my growing consternation blocking out most of her words, just as the desks the other day had blocked out most of her body. Our relationship seemed to be developing a peculiar truncated quality.

"I'm a rebel, is what I am," I heard her say at one point, "people just don't realize it."

I nodded, narrowing my eyes as if in appreciation of a subtly astute analysis, though I had no idea what had prompted her remark.

"Yes," I said, "I can see that."

"Does it bother you?"

"No."

"So I wasn't wrong, then, to do it?"

I racked my brains for an echo, a trace imprint of what she had just been talking about, but all I could think of were the words she had uttered a few minutes earlier—*he hit her with a steel bar*—that had sent me into this distracted state in the first place. A steel bar . . . I was trying to deny to myself the likelihood of a connection between this and the rod I had found under the desks in my office, but against this effort came wave upon wave of strange, surging apprehensiveness.

"Not at all," I hazarded in answer to Elaine's question. "I think you were absolutely right to do it."

She nodded: glad, apparently, of my approval for whatever it was she had done, but seemingly placed by it in some difficult new quandary:

"So what should I tell them?"

"Well . . . what do you want to tell them?"

"I'm not sure. Sometimes I almost feel like telling them to go take a running jump!"

"Then that's what you should do!"

So it continued: Elaine supplying the talk, me tuning out despite my best efforts to follow. At one point I realized from the way she was looking at me, and from a dim, lingering sense of a rising intonation at the end of the last phrase that had drifted by (no more intelligibly than the hum of the refrigerator), that she had just asked me another question.

"Well?" she said, after a longish pause.

It occurred to me that in my capacity as projected apparition, I was perhaps above having to observe the petty conventions of rational or continuous discourse. I could say or do whatever I felt like, and Elaine would adapt pliably to my whim.

I put my hand under her chin and drew her head toward mine. She seemed startled, but as I'd predicted, she acquiesced in the gesture. I kissed her lips, then probed into her mouth with my tongue. We were seated on her black-stained dining room chairs, a little too far apart to embrace, our conjoined heads forming an apex over the tile-floored space between us. A multitude of things tumbled about in my mind as we kissed. I tried to focus on the sweater-clad torso beside me and think of Carol. For a moment I felt almost present in the physical reality of what I was doing, but then the distractions impinged again: the letter I had never written; the steel rod I had mistaken for an innocent component of my office furniture. . . . Meanwhile, the kiss continued. Sooner or later, I supposed, I would catch up with it—find out what it meant to me, what it had accomplished, if anything. Right now it existed only for Elaine. Judging by the frantic vigor of her response, she was enjoying it.

"That's your answer," I said, pulling away.

I stood up. "And now I have to get going."

She blinked at me, baffled but unprotesting.

While we waited for my taxi, she became rapidly subdued. No doubt my erratic behavior had finally got to her. She had a large capacity for pain, I sensed, if also for the endurance of pain. There was something softly monumental about her, living out here by herself like a pioneer woman out on the plains. Though in all but body I was already halfway up Mulberry Street to the dark campus, my hand gripping the key to Room 106, my nerves preparing themselves for the shock of a possible encounter with a startled Trumilcik, I had enough regard for her to attempt a gracious exit.

"I'd like to see you again," I said.

"Would you?"

I put my arms around her.

"Let's go away somewhere, shall we? For a weekend?"

She nodded.

"I'll organize it," I said.

I kissed her again. This time I felt a wave of desire; unexpectedly powerful. I don't know why; perhaps the feelings of guilt and pity she'd succeeded in arousing in me had supplied the component missing before. With a familiar swarming sensation, my center of gravity shifted downward from my head. My mouth and hands, answerable to a new set of priorities, acquired a new boldness. I felt them slide over her breasts and down across her skirt to her groin.

She pulled back a little, registering the change.

"What are you doing?"

"This," I said with a smile, tumbling us both into the oatmeal denim couch. It was always amazing to me, the changes of consciousness that came over one at these moments. I felt abruptly free of inhibitions.

She gazed up at me with a look of helpless bewilderment.

"It's all right," I said.

"Is it?"

"We've been wanting this for a long time, haven't we?"

Even my voice sounded different, its timbre suddenly playful and brazen, as though I had entered a state of irrepressible good spirits; one that couldn't but be irresistibly infectious to anyone near me.

"I don't mean *just* this," I said, "but this too. . . ."

She looked at me, saying nothing.

I kissed her very gently on her lips and throat. She lay unresponsive, then turned her face from under mine.

"No?" I asked, grinning. "No?"

"No!" She said, with sudden firmness.

I kissed her again.

Frowning at me, she pushed me off her and stood up abruptly from the sofa. She looked extremely upset.

A little later I was striding up Mulberry Street, key prematurely in hand as I had envisaged, my mind plunging forward into the question of what exactly I should do with Trumilcik's rod when I retrieved it from under the desks.

Naturally my first thought was to take it to the police and tell them what I knew about Trumilcik. But as I imagined how my list of Trumilcik's manifestations might sound to a New York police detective, I began to have doubts. Someone who hadn't seen the bookmark, the phone bill, the coin, or the computer file in the first place might not find the disappearance of these things all that compelling. The hideout under the desks might look to them like nothing more than empty space. And to a person without the sophistication to connect a certain kind of womanizing with a capacity for homicidal misogyny, the presence of a steel rod there might seem less than significant. All in all, I realized I might be in danger of being politely dismissed as a lunatic.

For this reason I decided I would keep the rod myself; find a safe place to hide it until I had something more tangible to present alongside it.

In a sense what I discovered on entering my room was precisely that. Unfortunately, its tangibility was of a nature so violently unpleasant I couldn't even consider becoming the means of disclosing it to another human being. If ever there was a message vile enough to warrant the execution of its messenger, this was it. It lay on the desk where I had left my offering for Trumilcik, surrounded by smeared, torn-up pieces of paper. The money was gone: in its place, as if by some nightmarish reverse alchemy, a brown, pyramidal mound; raw and reeking, the nastiest gift one person can give another, so smolderingly dense in its physical reality it seemed to give the objects about it—books, papers, telephone, stapler—a quality of tentative abstraction.

Appalled, leaving the light off and the door open, I approached the coiled pile, which glistened horribly in the faint radiance of the campus lights.

It was on the blotter, at least, this dollop of antimatter; movable without the need for direct contact. The soiled bits of paper scrunched around it like netherworld origami were Amber's pages; what remained of them. I picked the blotter up; carried it steadily as I could so as not to be so much as fluttered against by the unclean crumpled scraps. To my left, the closed-together desks registered themselves on me with a dull pressure as I crossed back to the door and passed on into the corridor. If it is true that certain actions performed in the secular world have their true meaning elsewhere, in the world of the spirit, then this was surely one. I moved toward the men's room, trying hard to induce a state of imperviousness to what I was doing. It seemed a matter of some urgency not to let this event secure a place for itself in my psyche. It was night; I was alone; in a moment all evidence of its having occurred at all would be literally flushed away. As good, I told myself, as if it *hadn't* occurred at all. In the sepulchral dimness of the corridor, lit only by low-wattage night-lights at distant intervals, I could almost believe I wasn't really here; was elsewhere, dreaming this, as I did sometimes dream of such things.

In the men's room, between the rubber garbage bin and the toilet, I was able to dispose of everything, blotter included. I went back to my office. By now a heavy weariness had replaced my horror. I felt torn, demoralized. If Trumilcik was in there somewhere, then so be it. I turned on the light, opened the window to let out the lingering odor. Then I went to the desks, gave them a warning thump, and pulled them apart. He wasn't there.

Nor, however, was the steel rod.

Chapter 7

The next day I went into the department office at lunchtime to get my mail. Amber was there, working the photocopier. She looked at me drowsily. Her eyelids seemed literally weighted down by their brush of thick, cornsilk-colored lashes. For a moment I thought we might not have to speak. But under the surface torpor of her expression, a keener attentiveness began shoaling up towards me, and I felt once again the familiar agitated sense of having to account for myself as I stood before her.

"Listen, I—" I blustered, "I haven't had a chance to—to read your thing yet. . . ."

"Oh, no problem." Her voice was remote but soothing, like a phrase of otherworldly music drifting by on a breeze. She turned back to the photocopier.

There was a note in my mailbox. It was unsigned, and the words were in Latin:

Atrocissimum est Monoceros.

I didn't know what it meant, but its obvious hostility (a tauntingly opaque follow-up, I assumed, to last night's more crudely visceral assault) broke on me like a whiplash out from the dark, and I felt almost physically stung. I looked over at Amber; I wanted to say something, to whinny out an aggrieved protest and hear the reassurance of another human being's sympathetic outrage. On reflection, however, I realized Amber would hardly be an appropriate recipient for such an appeal. I stood there in silence, dazed, regretting for a moment (even as I acknowledged its importance) this unremitting obligation to hold oneself in check. I was gazing at her back: the obverse of the gold coin of herself. Wings of fine down caught the light at her long neck. Her shoulders were trim and straight in the soft blue sheathing of her top, crisscrossed by the ocher halter of her brushed cotton dungarees. Her willowy figure barely curved at the hips, almost as expressive as her face of things yet to awaken into the full articulation of themselves.

She turned around, catching my eye before I could look away. I felt sharply annoyed with myself—not for failing to take evasive action fast enough, but for ogling her like that in the first place. I was about to leave the room when I heard her say softly:

"So you did know Barbara."

"I'm sorry?"

"You did know Barbara Hellermann."

"No . . ."

"But you were in Portland with her."

Amber's blue-sleeved arm pointed languidly over to a poster on the notice board. Distantly alarmed, I strolled across the room, as nonchalantly as I could.

The poster was for a week-long interdisciplinary graduate seminar on gender studies at the Portland State University campus. Among the fifteen or so guest speakers listed were myself and Barbara Hellermann. Looking at it, I felt a distinct but as yet unlocatable feeling of danger, which I see in retrospect was my first intimation of the large antagonisms I had unwittingly aroused.

"What's this doing up here?" I said. "It's three years out of date."

"I have no idea."

"How strange. Well perhaps I did meet her. I don't remember."

"She was my teacher here in my junior year."

"Oh."

I was about to tear the poster down when I thought that might strike Amber as odd. Instead I merely shrugged my shoulders and left the room.

Later, when nobody was there, I went back and discreetly removed the poster. Taking it into my office, I examined it closely. It looked genuine enough, not that I would have been able to tell if someone had forged it.

Perhaps, I thought, it had been left up there on the notice board all this time, and Amber pointing it out to me today, the very day after I had learned of Barbara Hellermann's murder, was merely a chance event; the kind that occurs when you learn a word you've never come across in your life, only to hear it repeated in an unrelated context almost immediately after. And perhaps, in that case, Barbara Hellermann really had been in Portland when I was there, and I simply hadn't taken note of her. There had been an organized dinner, I remembered, and a muddy walk through a forest of wild salmonberries and Douglas fir to a spectacular waterfall above the Columbia River. I had given my paper—part of a mini-symposium entitled "Engineering the New Male." Other than that we'd been left to our own devices. I wasn't very sociable—I spent most of my free time on the phone to Carol (who only wasn't with me because she was so afraid of flying she never went anywhere she didn't absolutely have to go), and wishing I was back in New York with her. So it was possible that Barbara had been there, and that we simply hadn't registered each other. Possible, then, that the poster was genuine, and that it had been up on the notice board for three years without my taking it in. Possible.

Nevertheless, I brought the poster home with me and threw it into the incinerator.

After that I took my old prep school Latin dictionary down from its shelf in the living room and translated the note. At once I found my investigation (as it had unequivocally become by now) of Trumilcik lurching in an altogether unexpected direction.

Chapter 8

Watery, blinking eyes set in puffy tissue—too raw-looking and vulnerable to gaze at for long without discomfort. Thin, curving nose with scimitar-shaped nostrils. Mouth tight with old habits of suppression—frustration, disappointment, physical pain. . . .

Ill-at-ease in his life, one had to surmise; my father.

A high street pharmacist's son with intellectual pretensions, who'd left university after one year to take a pharmacy diploma and run the family business when his own father died.

My mother was working behind the till: eighteen, with aspirations of her own.

She was pregnant with me by the time my father realized how much he disliked standing in a white coat filling out prescriptions for the wheezing, flatulent, swollen-footed, stye-eyed, hemorrhoidal denizens of Shepherds Bush. My mother urged him, so she claimed, to sell the business. "I wanted him to become a BOAC pilot," she told me, "but instead he had to make himself ill with that idiotic book of his."

Shortly after I was born, he had embarked on a history of

pharmacology, a *magnum opus* intended to spirit him out of the Goldhawk Road, that endless stretch of secondhand appliance shops and dismal pubs, into the fragrant cloisters of some venerable old university. Lacking what he called "formal discipline" (a phrase my mother used to repeat with an inimitable mixture of piety and acid irony), he had quickly started floundering in the morass of his own research. But rather than give up, he had thrown himself into the task ever more obstinately, lashing himself into a daily foment of wasted effort. The picture my mother's words conveyed was one of Sisyphean tragedy undercut by baleful pathos—an ambitious, untutored mind hammering at its limitations as if at the wall of its own skull, in the effort to turn the columns of books and notes rising around him like so many stalagmites into a polished monument of erudition, such as he imagined the academic publishers he had his eye on might be impressed by. "Instead all he produced was a headache," my mother would conclude dryly, "poor man."

As a matter of fact, she wasn't entirely right. After his first bout with the brain tumor, he appeared to have made a strategic concession to mortality, turning some of his notes into self-contained articles and sending them out to learned journals. The mills of those organs grinding no doubt even more slowly than usual through his unaccredited submissions, he was dead by the time the editors of a couple of them informed him they would be pleased to carry his observations in future issues. But in this way his labors, which were no doubt all he would have cared to be remembered by, did at least come to fruition.

And it was through these too—these posthumously published articles—that he unexpectedly acquitted himself as a father, procuring for the son he barely knew, a wife.

The first inkling I had of her existence was an envelope sent from Cambridge, Massachusetts, to the Manchester Society of

Apothecaries' quarterly journal, forwarded from there to my mother's former home, and from there back across the Atlantic to my apartment on Horatio Street. The letter inside was addressed to my father. Carol had read one of his articles in the course of her own researches at Harvard and wondered if the volume-in-progress mentioned in the contributor's note had ever been completed.

She wrote by hand, in blue ink on cream-colored card. Her writing was neat and stylish, done with a thick italic nib, so that it looked a little like something from an illuminated manuscript; but lively too—the letters pennanted with so many jibs and serifs they seemed to be fluttering in their own private breeze.

I wrote back telling her that my father had died before completing the volume, and enclosing copies of his other published articles. She was welcome, I added, to come and look through his papers anytime she happened to be in New York.

A few weeks later she phoned from Cambridge to take me up on my offer.

She came to my studio on a chilly afternoon in March, wrapped in a long, royal blue, capelike coat with a gold-lined hood. I showed her my father's papers and went out, telling her I would leave her in peace for a few hours. She thanked me and sat at the desk by the big steel window that looked out over the West River.

The sun was low in the sky when I came back. Carol was in the same posture as I had left her in earlier, apparently rapt. "This is fascinating material," she said. "Your father had an original mind."

I didn't want to admit that I had never actually looked at his papers, and I turned the conversation to her own work instead.

She was writing a doctoral thesis, she told me, on ideas of purity and pollution in medieval and early Renaissance Europe.

One avenue of her researches had led her into the subject of poisons and their antidotes, and it was here, delving into the medieval pharmacopoeia of bezoar stones, griffin claws, *terra sigillata*, oil of scorpions, powdered smaragdus, and so on, that she had chanced on my father's articles.

What interested her were certain paradoxes at the heart of medieval thought, such as the equally held belief in the curative powers of both extremely pure and extremely impure substances, and an apparent ambivalence when it came to deciding which of the two categories any given substance belonged to.

I stood by her as we talked—there was no furniture other than the futon, the desk, and the chair she was sitting in. I'd deliberately kept the place bare since moving in. I liked that ringing emptiness—the sense of promise not yet unfulfilled—you get from a new room you haven't yet colonized with your things. Against that bareness, Carol's presence was all the more vivid: a brand-new, gleaming-eyed human phenomenon to take account of. She wore no jewelry or makeup, I noticed. Her straight, almost black hair fell thick and smooth around her face, shiny as a helmet. Her mouth was small but full, with curving shadows at the corners of her lips that gave her expression of cool asperity a barely accountable mirthfulness. She didn't flirt, but she didn't withhold herself either. When I looked at her she held my gaze candidly, even challengingly, as though curious to test my interest, or my nerve. Her unadorned wrists and hands were finely articulated—long-fingered, with concise, pliant joints that had their own look of high intelligence.

The sun slid down behind the Hoboken smokestacks. At that hour the river looks taut and self-contained, as if a scooped handful wouldn't run, but wobble on your palm like mercury, burning coldly.

I was single then, and at a stage where I was no longer satisfied by the brief relationships and casual flings that my love life so far had consisted of. I had come to realize that I no longer wanted a "lover," or a "girlfriend"; that I wanted a *wife*. I wanted something durable about me—a fortress and a sanctuary. I wanted a woman whom I could love—as a character in a book I'd read put it—*sincerely, without irony, and without resignation*. I had been observing a self-imposed celibacy as I waited for the right woman to come along: partly so as not to be entangled when I met her, but also, more positively, in order to create in myself the state of receptiveness and high sensitization I considered necessary for an auspicious first meeting. I believed that human relations were capable of partaking in a certain mystery; that under the right conditions something larger than the sum of what each individual brought with them, could transfuse itself into the encounter, elevating it and permanently shielding it from the grinding destructiveness of everyday life. And just such a mystery, such a baptism-in-love, was what I felt to be heavily and sweetly impending as I stood beside Carol in my room that afternoon. I knew almost nothing of her, and yet it seems to me I knew as much about her at that moment as I ever came to learn in the years that followed. The outward circumstances of her existence were immaterial to the intensity of what passed between us as we paused in our conversation there, high above the river. She could have been brought up in Timbuktu rather than Palo Alto, could have had five brothers in show business rather than two sisters in medical school; she might have summered with an uncle in the Rockies rather than an aunt in Cape Cod, had a fear of spiders instead of a fear of flying. . . . These details, though charmed because they concerned *her*, added little to the essential, radiant mutual disclosure that occurred in that moment.

In silence we watched a barge glide seaward on the gold and mauve water, tumbling curled shavings of foam from its stern.

"That's some view you have," Carol remarked, turning to me with a smile.

As she looked at me, the firm, clear outline of her beautiful face was lit by the trapezoid of dark yellow light coming in through the window.

I had the sense of being inscribed on, etched into, by the sight.

The battered suitcase containing my father's papers was now back in the hall closet. Even though I had gone to the trouble of bringing it out here to the States, I had always felt an odd, almost narcotic weariness at the thought of going through its contents. But whatever obscure private taboo that weariness represented, it was overruled now by a sense of urgent practical necessity.

What first caught my eye when I opened the suitcase had nothing to do with my father: bristling all over the piles of manuscript were brightly colored little arrow-shaped clips that Carol had used to mark passages she wanted to return to.

She always studded whatever she was reading with these things: they were part of her permanent retinue of physical objects, like her tortoiseshell comb or her italic-nibbed silver pen. They were the first things of hers I had seen in months; the first physical evidence that she had once shared my life in this apartment, and the sight of them had a powerful effect on me. She had left something of herself behind after all! Red, green, yellow, blue . . . they teemed under my eyes like shiny winged insects. I felt simultaneously the sharp anguish of her loss and the passionate warmth that even a passing thought of her had always been capable of arousing in me. It would have been easy to spend the rest of the evening sitting there adrift on these bits of plastic, thinking about her, and I had to make a deliberate effort to turn my attention instead to the immense piles of yellowed manuscript into which they had been inserted.

Letting Carol's markers guide me through the pages, I read with a kind of detached attentiveness, noting the quirks of my father's mind, the strengths and weaknesses of his thought processes, the turns of phrase he favored, with guarded pleasure and even an occasional moment of wry self-recognition. He was evidently nervous of advancing an argument without first marshaling an army of authorities to support him, then further reinforcing it with an array of obscure technical terms and foreign phrases—insecurities I had noticed in my own work. And like me, he had a preference for lateral, associative movement over the forward march of sequential narrative, which was no doubt one reason why he had never completed his work. Fragments of chapters ramified into multiple digressions that subdivided into footnotes that, like the cells of regenerative limbs, miraculously grew into chapters in their own right.

At one point Carol's markers became much more densely clustered. My own interest sharpened in sympathy. Here was a passage on the prevalence of poisoning in the courts of the Borgias and the Burgundians. A lengthy disquisition followed, on the widely held belief in the efficacy of animal horns as antidotes and prophylactics. Stag horns, rams' horns, hartshorn; hollowed as goblets, shaved, powdered, dissolved in water or wine, worn as amulets; horns of the antelope, the rhinoceros, the Plate River *pyrassouppi*, were listed and discussed, their lore and applications summarized, all in a frenzy of deferential nods to Lucretius, Odell Shepard, the *Pharmacopoeia Medico-Chymica*, while the little sharp arrows of Carol's attention rained down on almost every line.

Of all the horns, I read, the alicorn was universally deemed the most powerful. Alicorn? Ah, the horn of the unicorn.

I knew that Carol had gone back to the manuscript a couple of years after first reading it, when she began her book on the medieval cult of the Virgin Mary. She had wanted to check what my father had had to say about the myth of the unicorn hunt, where the creature is lured into captivity by a virgin before being killed.

"The creature never lived," wrote my father in an extended footnote, "yet there is an abundance of evidence for it, and for several centuries the leading minds of their day believed in its existence. Cuvier and Livingstone were among those still prepared to countenance the possibility of an animal with a single horn in its forehead, as late as the nineteenth century. True Unicorn Horn (*verum cornu monocerotis*) not only had the power to cleanse sullied waters, but was also said to sweat in the presence of poison. For this reason it was worth ten times its weight in gold. . . ."

I had the sense now that I was getting somewhere, as far as tracking down the source of my anonymous note. I was aware too, without quite knowing why, that far from reassuring me, this was making me feel distinctly uncomfortable.

"Two explanations exist," the footnote continued, "for the medicinal action of the horn. Polar opposites, they go to the heart not only of the principal paradox in early theories of healing, but also of the ambivalent nature of the unicorn itself. Teeth, hooves, and especially horns, were believed to concentrate the essences of the creatures they came from. In the case of the single horn of a unicorn, this concentrate would of course be twice as strong as in, say, the twinned antlers of a stag.

"Depending on whether an authority believed the essence of a unicorn to be benign or evil, its effect would be explained either by the doctrine of allopathy, where a virtuous substance is thought to counteract a venomous one, or else by the doctrine of homeopathy, which declares that 'like cures like' (*similia similibus curantur*), and that the only way to detect or disarm a poison is to place it in the diminishing context of something even more poisonous than itself.

"Allegorists wishing to see the unicorn as a symbol of Christ naturally adhered to the allopathic doctrine, which held that the horn was the ultimate pure substance. The Christianized Greek Bestiary, for example, gives an explicitly religious version of the Cleansing of the Waters, or 'Water Conning,' illustrated in the second of the Unicorn Tapestries at the Cloisters Museum in New York, asserting that the creature makes the sign of the cross over the water with his horn before dipping it in.

"Homeopathists, on the other hand, regard the horn as the ultimate toxic substance, believing that it sweats in the presence of other poisons because of a desire to mingle with its own kind. The pharmacist Laurent Catelan, noting that horned animals like to eat poisonous substances of all kinds, deduced that a powerful toxic residue of these substances must be stored in their horns.

"Far from Christlike, the unicorn of this school is an aggressive, highly unsociable monster. In pictures of Noah's Ark or Adam naming the Beasts, it usually has the distinction of being the only creature without a mate. Aelian is alone among the more reputable authorities in mentioning the existence of female unicorns. 'The males fight not just among themselves,' he declares, 'but they war against the females too, pushing the struggle to the death.' Maddened by the enormous pain caused by the toxins distilled in his horn, the unicorn—'this ryght cruell beast' as John of Trevisa calls him—'fyghtyth ofte with the Elyphaunt and woundyth & styketh him in the wombe.' *Atrocissimum est Mono-*

ceros begins Julius Solinus's description, put into English by Arthur Golding: 'But the cruellest is the Unicorn, a monster that belloweth horriblie.' "

Monoceros: a unicorn.

I looked again at the note I had found in my mailbox:

Atrocissimum est Monoceros.

I had half-expected this, but having tracked the phrase to its source, it seemed after all that it solved nothing, or if it did, in doing so merely opened more perplexing questions. How could the phrase have transmigrated from my father's papers to my mailbox at work? Until now, Carol was the only living person who had read the manuscript, but it was inconceivable that Carol would stoop to anything so puerile as the delivering of cryptic, anonymous notes. Equally inconceivable was the idea that she and this man Trumilcik could somehow be in contact, let alone in *cahoots*. Carol in her universe of museums, academic conferences, cultured conversation; Trumilcik, whom one could only imagine now as some kind of shambling maniac, a street ghoul lost in a private labyrinth of paranoia and scatographic rage . . . It wasn't possible! I seemed to be up against something impenetrably mysterious. My father . . . Carol . . . Trumilcik . . . Broken sequences seemed to radiate out from me in all directions. Elaine . . . Barbara Hellermann . . . Chains with missing links . . . My mind was whirling!

I poured myself a drink and tried to calm down. There were papers to grade, new publications to catch up on. I made an attempt to settle down to an hour or two of work before dinner, but I was too restless to concentrate. I drifted into the kitchen, took the cold leftovers of a Chinese takeout from the fridge, and turned on the radio. A commentator was talking about the pos-

sible impeachment of the President. For obvious reasons this
was a subject that interested me greatly, and I tried to pay
attention. But before I could even tell which side of the question the commentator was on, a name came into my head,
appearing there with such a burst of illumination that I said it
aloud:

Blumfeld!

A moment later I was turning the apartment upside down:
emptying drawers, peering under the sofa, tearing apart the new
junk piles that had risen all over the floor like molehills since I'd
last tidied.

If the Blumfeld actress (I didn't know her name) was indeed
the actress who had come to dinner with Carol's colleague on the
night of that disastrous outing to the Plymouth Rock, then from
Carol to Trumilcik, by way of her colleague and this actress,
there existed one of those ley-lines of human connection, as significant or meaningless, depending on your point of view, as
their geographic counterpart. From *my* point of view, skeptical
as I was of such things, I was sufficiently anxious for answers by
now that I felt it imperative to explore even the remotest possibility of elucidation.

After an exhaustive search I still hadn't found what I was
looking for. But I did find something else. It seemed my propen-
sity for absentminded slips and lapses, my gift for *parapraxis*,
could work in my favor on occasion: instead of throwing away
the office phone bill with the nighttime call on it, as I'd assumed
I had, I had apparently brought it home and carefully hidden it
from myself on a small cupboard next to my desk, under a box
full of floppy disks. There it lay, as though it had been calmly
amusing itself all this time, waiting for me to rediscover it. There
was the number, there the precise time it was dialed: 2:14 A.M.
The call had lasted less than one minute.

A machine picked up when I dialed. There was no message; just a beep. I hung up.

I then went out—first to the cybercafé, hoping to find the playbill with the actress's name on it still up on the wall. It was gone. Given the prevailing pattern of disappearances, I had no reason to expect anything less. I left, heading east and north to the still-ungentrified blocks fringing the FDR Drive; the roads a patchwork of cobble and tar, cracked sidewalks tilting from frost heaves; strangely reassuring, all of it, as though it spoke to one's own impending obsolescence.

I should have expected this too: the synagogue windows, merely broken before, were now boarded up. The front door was padlocked with a heavy chain. I went down the steps to the scuffed metal door of the basement theater. There was no chain, but the door seemed firmly locked. I gave it a kick, more out of a sense of what seemed expected by its battered face than anything else. To my surprise, it opened.

It was pitch-dark inside. The streetlight barely penetrated down here. I waited in the doorway till my eyes adjusted to what little did. Ahead of me to the left, a silvery brushstroke marked the handle of the double-door into the auditorium. To my right, a rectangle of more absolute blackness than the background must have been the table. I took a step toward it.

Immediately I caught a familiar smell: the acrid male rankness I had smelled in Trumilcik's hideout. My body prickled with alarm. I would have retreated, had my move toward the table not revealed an unevenness in the straight-edged blackness of its surface, just where the pile of programs had been the last time I was here. In three quick steps, I reached it and grabbed what did indeed feel like the shiny, folded paper I had been searching for in my apartment. As I turned to leave, I felt a kind of raging force rearing up toward me out of the darkness. I was aware of this in a purely animal way; before I saw or even heard the immense, bearded figure lurch across the doorway in my direction. It was the only time I did see him; pale and tattered, stinking of dereliction, his gray hair thick and flailing, his copious, rabbinical beard matted with filth. I bolted for the door. As I did, something rock-hard erupted out from him, smashing into my face. In memory, the gesture has a peculiar, deliberate judiciousness about it; a large accounting of things, condensed into a single, hieratic movement. My momentum took me crashing on out through the door. I managed to stagger up the steps to the sidewalk and keep moving until I realized I was not being pursued. At that point I collapsed in the entranceway of an apartment building, bleeding and trembling.

I still had the paper in my hand. It was the program: that at least had been accomplished. *Blumfeld, an Elderly Bachelor*; adapted for the stage by Bogomil Trumilcik. With M. K. Schroeder as Blumfeld.

Schroeder ... *Doctor* Schroeder, I thought, smiling as I remembered the check I had sent Dr. Schrever, then wincing with pain from the smile.

At home I found her listing in the phone book: M. K. Schroeder, 156 Washington Avenue. Again, a machine picked up, though on this one there was a voice: *Leave a message for Melody after the beep*. Melody ... how could I have forgotten such a name? Melody Schroeder. I left my own name and number and asked her to call me.

For good measure, I tried the other number again; again to no avail.

The whole of the left side of my face was a livid bruise; swollen and excruciatingly tender.

Chapter 9

I hadn't seen Elaine since our evening together at her house. I hadn't been avoiding her, but I hadn't been seeking her out either, and I suspected the same was true of her as regards myself. Things had ended on a troubled note, and we both needed time to take stock of what was happening between us.

On my part, I was unsure whether to attribute the sudden wave of desire that had taken hold of me to the discovery of a genuine feeling for Elaine, as I had at the time, or to some narrower, more opportunistic carnal impulse.

Had I felt at the time that it was the latter, I surely wouldn't have attempted to end the evening the way I did, in that flurry of grabbing and groping. I did what I did because I sincerely believed I had finally uncovered feelings in myself that reciprocated Elaine's, and that to make love was the most natural thing for us to do.

Clearly I was wrong, and I accept the blame for that, though I made the mistake in good faith. One is always somewhat in the dark in these matters; as much about one's own feelings as the other person's, and a certain amount of trial and error is inevitable. I felt sure that Elaine would understand this after she had had some time to reflect, and I remained optimistic about the possibilities for our relationship.

On the Thursday of the following week, Roger convened our committee for another emergency meeting. Zena Sayeed had spoken to Candida Johanssen, and the girl had agreed to make a formal complaint of sexual harassment against Bruno.

I expected to see Elaine at the meeting, and I went there determined to greet her with a friendly face—as friendly as my bruises would allow—and to suggest lunch after, if the opportunity arose.

I was surprised, then, when the meeting was about to begin and she still hadn't shown up.

I was on the point of asking where she was when I thought better of it. An instinct for caution was beginning to censor even the most innocent-seeming remarks at this time. There was also the fact that with the left side of my face looking like a slice of raw ox liver, I had no wish to draw any unnecessary attention to myself.

My question was asked for me, however, by the fifth member of our committee, a mild-mannered biologist named Tony Ardito.

"You didn't hear?" Roger answered him. "Her brother called in for her last week. She went to visit him in Iowa and got in a car crash in Sioux City. She's in the hospital with head injuries."

"Oh my gosh!"

"Yep. She's on indefinite leave."

"Boy!"

There was a pause in which it seemed to be tacitly agreed among us that further discussion of our missing member would be inappropriate, and Roger began to address the matter at hand.

For the second time in a week I found myself in a situation

where I was increasingly unable to concentrate on what was going on. The news of this accident, not to mention Elaine's trip to Iowa, was a shock, but I was aware that under my simple response of surprise was a more restless, agitated feeling, as though there were something about the information that made me unable to secure it inside me in a stable position. I felt like a child trying very hard to believe something that won't quite settle within the limits of her or his credulousness.

Earlier that week I had done something I would never have imagined doing in the days before the name Trumilcik entered my consciousness: I had looked up private investigators in the Yellow Pages, with a view to finding an address for the number he had called from my office. Just glancing down the list of names; the Sentinels and Warriors, the Bureaus, Corporations, Networks, and Associates, with their bulleted services—*Digital Lie Detection, Male and Female Armed Agents, Matrimonial Evidence, Nanny Surveillance*—had made me feel as though I'd been waylaid into some realm of existence as absurdly, shabbily gothic as the buildings I worked in. For a moment it seemed to me that I would do better, after all, to ignore Trumilcik and all his maneuvers; his notes and gifts, his pettily vindictive intrusions; just go on living my life as if he didn't exist. Nothing excites a bully more than signs of submission in his victim, and it was surely submissive of me to allow my actions to be dictated to me by Trumilcik's. I was about to put the phone book away when I'd caught sight of my bruised face in the mirror, and at once all the latent violence clinging like a dark fog around each of his manifestations seemed to gather into a single louring cloud of evil intent, and I realized after all that I would be well advised at this point to take whatever initiative I could.

The man who answered the phone at Crane, Coleman Associates—a name I picked out for its relative untheatricality—had sounded reassuringly businesslike. It wasn't hard, he said, to reverse-access an address from a listed number, and he quoted a reasonable-sounding price for doing so.

I gave him the number and my credit card details. A little later he called back to tell me that the number was *un*listed, and that this was going to make the job more expensive. He gave me a price more than four times the original. Uneasy, wondering if I was being taken for a ride, I told him to go ahead. The next morning he called to say he'd traced the address. There was an odd, unctuous quality in his voice that hadn't been there before. In view of the nature of this address, Lawrence, he had said, he was going to have to add a surcharge of two hundred dollars to his original quote.

I told him I didn't understand.

"Let's say you're paying for the risk we're taking here with our license, Lawrence, and, uh, you're guaranteeing a level of confidentiality for yourself."

"I still don't understand."

"It's a shelter, Mr. Miller," he said, "for victims of domestic abuse. They're very protective about their addresses, those places."

It took me a moment to understand that I was being black-mailed. A cry of indignant rage almost burst out of me, but again, like an invisible muzzle, my newfound instinct for caution had kept my mouth shut. I could make my complaint later; write to whatever governing body licensed these outfits, when all this unpleasantness was over and no unhelpful ambiguities could attach themselves to my interest in the address of such a shelter.

"All right," I snapped, "I'll pay the surcharge."

He gave me the address. I looked at a map and saw that the town it was in—a place called Corinth—was upstate a hundred and fifty miles or so. But having gone to the trouble and expense

of finding this out, I'd fallen into an odd state of inertia, as if
I'd prematurely exhausted my interest in self-preservation, and I
had done nothing to follow up on the information.

Now, though, here at the meeting, with the news of Elaine's
disappearance bobbing and shifting in my mind, I felt again the
folly of not pursuing any hint that might shed light on Trumilcik. For reasons I couldn't yet fully articulate, the two discover-
ies—Elaine's crash (her *alleged* crash, I was already calling it)
and Trumilcik's connection to a shelter for victims of domestic
abuse—converged in my mind on a point of obscure but urgently
galvanizing dread. It seemed to me that it would be a good idea
to pay a visit to this shelter. How to get inside it, and what to do
there even if I could, was less clear.

The meeting—in effect a dismissal proceeding—passed like a
muffled dream under these preoccupations. No doubt the minutes I took were as assiduous as ever, but I was barely conscious
of what I was writing. Of the actual confrontation with Bruno I
recall little other than a general sense of his disdainful refusal to
defend himself against Candida Johanssen's accusations, and his
apparent indifference to the impending termination of his career
(something self-consciously British about his laconic posture, I
remember dimly feeling, as though in his mind he was Raleigh
in the Tower, or Sir Thomas More on the scaffold, unflappably
tying his own blindfold: *See me safe up, and for my coming down
let me shift for myself . . .*).

I do, however, retain a vivid impression of his physical presence in the room. He was wearing his thick black coat, the
one with the slit at the back, and he declined to remove it. His
long legs—hind legs, I find myself tempted to call them—were
sheathed in skin-tight black drainpipes; tight as an Elizabethan's
doublet and hose. All he lacked was a codpiece. It struck me, I

remember, that there was even something indecent about his face. Handsome as it was, its very handsomeness was of a kind that made you want to avert your eye, as though, having been drawn to it by an apparent fineness, you suddenly realized you were looking at a body part that should have been covered. I thought of the previous meeting; how I had sat there taking notes with one hand, while my other gently kneaded Elaine's thigh under the table, and I felt the irony of a situation that had positioned me on one side of this table, obliged by convention to conceal a perfectly legitimate consensual act, while setting Bruno, on the other, free to flaunt that naked knot of sense organs that devolved, when you regarded it for more than a moment, into the embodiment of an obscene proposition.

Thinking of him now, I feel more than ever the rightness of the great repudiation of masculinity that so many of us in academe consider the supreme contribution of the humanities in our time. Masculinity in its old, feral, malevolent guise, that is; unadapted masculinity worthy of nothing more than its own inevitable extinction. I can almost see a furry tail waving between the split skirts of Bruno's coat as he walks out of the room. . . .

He turned to me from the door:

"Where'd you get the black eye from, Lawrence? Did someone put up a fight?"

"I slipped on ice," I muttered in reply to the first part of his question. The second part I didn't understand.

As it happened, Bruno's words proved unexpectedly helpful. By reminding me of my appearance while I was in the midst of all my other preoccupations, they gave me an idea I might not otherwise have had.

Returning to my office after the meeting, I locked the door behind me and opened the closet. There, hanging on the peg, were Barbara Hellermann's maroon beret and her dry cleaning.

I took down the beret and put it on my head.

Modest as this gesture was, it filled me with a strange excitement, as though a minor adjustment to some telescopic instrument had abruptly swung a whole new galaxy of possibilities into view.

The hat was a good fit. It felt warm and very comfortable. In the mirror it sat softly on my lank blond hair, looking only a little strange. With my high cheekbones and smooth chin, I reminded myself of some film actress from the forties, the bruise and black eye not altogether ruining the effect. I could pass for a female member of the French Resistance, I thought; heroically holding out after being beaten by her captors.

Or I could pass for a more modern kind of heroine: a battered woman, for instance, summoning up the courage to escape from her abuser.

I went back to the closet for the dry cleaning. Under the wrapper I could see a fawn-colored jerkin-style jacket with a quilted lining, and a brown skirt of heavy, woven yarn.

A powerful, almost gleeful sense of purpose came into me as I folded these into my briefcase along with the maroon beret. I felt that I was finally on the attack.

At home I dialed the shelter. The machine picked up as usual. This time I left a message.

Chapter 10

It had snowed in the night, but now it was raining. The traffic, solid from the Port Authority, sizzled through the slush along the West River, which was all but choked with its own traffic of car-sized, mud-colored chunks of ice.

I was on a Trailways bus bound for Corinth.

I was wearing Barbara's clothes, along with a polo neck sweater, and some women's shoes and wool tights I'd bought to complete the outfit. In my initial excitement at this plan, I had assumed it would be something that I, of all people, should have been able to execute without psychic cost; with even a certain professional enthusiasm. I had told myself that a journey in women's clothing would be a learning—an *empowering*—experience; something I might even ask my male students to try as an exercise. I remembered reading that Siberian shamans would sometimes undergo a symbolic transformation into women as a part of their journey into the spirit realm. Perhaps I would come back like them with healing or prophetic visions, or, like Tiresias, with a completed knowledge of what it was to be human.

What I hadn't counted on was the tremendous resistance of one's mass of unconscious prejudices—one's gender-soul, if I can call it that—to this kind of disturbance. Stepping out onto the street in these clothes, I had felt an abrupt, cascading sense of inward collapse; almost a feeling of shame, as if I were wearing this long brown skirt, these chrome-buckled pumps, under duress; as a punishment for some crime I'd committed without knowing it.

As I'd turned onto Avenue A, I had seen Mr. Kurwen walking toward me with a black patch over his missing eye. All my remaining strength seemed to go out of me as we approached each other. I wanted very badly not to be recognized by him. Despite my own knowledge that what I was doing was both rational and necessary, I felt unequal to the savage hilarity I knew my transformation would arouse in such a man. His good eye stared hard at me as we came close. I don't know if he recognized me, but for a moment I felt cornered and utterly defenseless.

At the Port Authority I had gone without thinking into the men's room to pee. A man in a suit, still fastening his fly as he turned from the urinal, had looked at me, startled. Catching sight of myself in the mirror, I realized he was looking at a woman in a maroon beret who was apparently about to approach the porcelain stalls, and I beat a hasty retreat to the women's room; mortified, and again strangely humiliated. Here, as I washed my hands at the sink, a white-haired old lady had tut-tutted sympathetically at me in the mirror. "Boyfriend?" she'd murmured, gesturing at my bruises. I hesitated a moment, then nodded. She shook her head with a sigh.

I'd felt even worse after that. Aside from abusing the woman's sympathy, this little misappropriation of female suffering seemed to deepen the reality of what I was doing. To my general despondency, a new, sharply particular kind of demoralization was added: I had just stepped into character, I realized. I was a battered woman.

Over the bridge and all along the Palisades the rain kept the traffic at the same funereal adagio. We lumbered off onto the throughway. Mountains appeared; nothing on them but the endless rolling smoke of winter trees, barely distinguishable from the clouds above them or the gray explosions of rain in between.

The vastness of America, the great volumes of space in which one's existence has no meaning to anyone or anything, is overpowering at times like this. If you're alone, you feel your aloneness as an almost physical encumbrance. An acute homesickness seizes you; unballasted, in my case, by any sense of where home might be. To be traveling through the rain, dressed as a woman, with a broken face, from a place where I had almost no human connections left, to one where I had none at all, seemed suddenly pitiful. There was a certain margin of tolerance, I felt; an elastic limit stretching only so far from the warm centers of human society. Step beyond it, and you couldn't count on being gathered back in. And it wouldn't necessarily be society that kept you out, but something in yourself; some unassimilable new singularity making you unfit, *by your own judgment,* for the company of your fellow creatures.

At a rest stop on Route 9—a senses-jangling temple of commerce set down by what appeared to be primeval forest—I sat with a cup of bile-colored coffee, staring through the rain-streaming glass, thinking I could disappear out of my life without a ripple; could just get up and walk out there into those dripping oaks and pines, and vanish. . . . There was something appealing about the idea; soothing almost. I pictured myself hiding out there somewhere; huddled in a damp cave or pine-bough shelter over a smoking heap of dead leaves. . . .

The reverie must have connected with some deep wish or fantasy. I was so lost in it that it took several attempts for the voice I was hearing beside me to get through.

"Ma'am, we're ready to leave now. Ma'am?"

I turned and saw that the voice belonged to the bus driver, and that she was addressing me.

"I'm sorry," I murmured.

"Oh, no problem." She smiled at me, her eye lingering a moment on my hurt cheek.

I followed her back to the bus, checking the hang of my skirt as I crossed the forecourt through the rain.

Two hours later we came to a small city on a plain under jagged hills. A water tower in the form of a giant, inverted teardrop bore the legend CORINTH.

At the bus station, a short, overweight man with a mustache paused by my seat as I reached for my suitcase.

"Want help there, lady?"

I thought I would make myself less conspicuous by accepting than refusing.

"Oh . . . thank you."

He lifted the suitcase down and insisted on carrying it out of the bus for me.

"Where're you headed?"

I opened my umbrella, wondering if there was some special way women did this.

"To my girlfriend's house," I said.

"What part of town? I'll give you a ride."

"That's all right, thanks."

"Really—it'd be no trouble."

"That's all right, thank you. I'll get a cab." I turned from him.

"Hey, wait—"

He was wagging his finger at me, his small eyes twinkling

roguishly. I thought he must have seen through my disguise, and that I was now going to have to publicly prove I was a woman.

But "You're *British*, right?" was all he said.

Relieved, I confessed that I was.

"I have a cousin in Dorsetshire."

"Oh."

"Do you know that area?"

"A little."

"He's a mechanic, Russell Thorpe. Russ Thorpe?"

"I don't . . . I haven't met him."

"Too bad, I think you'd like him. Listen, you want a drink? Just, you know, go to a bar, have a couple cocktails?"

He was friendly enough, even quite jolly, with his fat man's awareness of his own slightly comical ungainliness. But the mere fact of his presumption that he could talk to me, make suggestions bearing on the disposition of my own person, was startlingly hard to take.

"Oh . . . no . . . I have to get to my friend's house."

I smiled appeasingly at him and hurried away.

"What's the matter, I'm too skinny for you?" I heard him call with a chuckle as I went off in search of a taxi.

The shelter was on a quiet street of run-down old mansions. It was in better repair than most of them, with a new-looking red roof and warm, mustard-colored clapboard walls. A tall fence jutted from either side of it, enclosing a backyard from which I could hear the voices of children playing in the drizzle. There was nothing to tell you the place was a shelter until you climbed the porch steps to the front door and saw a security camera in a steel cage staring down at you.

I pressed the buzzer, showing my face to the camera. The heavy door clicked open and I carried my suitcase into a warm, light-filled vestibule that smelled of clean laundry and floor polish.

Strollers and outdoor boots were lined neatly against the walls, and over the stairway was a children's collage of a rainbow with the word WELCOME dangling from it in foil letters.

A woman was smiling at me from the top of the stairs.

"Marlene?"

I nodded. I had given my name as Marlene Winters in the brief conversation I had had with the woman who'd returned my call the previous day.

"C'mon up. We've been expecting you. I'm Josephine."

I climbed the stairs and Josephine gave me a light hug, look-ing over my bruises with a brief sympathetic wince that dis-solved back into a smile.

"You need something for that, honey? An ice pack, maybe? You sure? Be no trouble to fix you one. . . ."

She led me into an office where I filled out a form with false information and signed an agreement not to disclose the address of the shelter to anyone I knew.

"We have all kind of counseling and legal services for you when you're good and ready," Josephine said, "but I'm guessing right now you probably could use a good rest more than any-thing else. Am I right?"

I nodded. Though I had practiced using a higher-pitched voice than normal, I had thought it would be wise to minimize speak-ing altogether.

"I'll show you your room."

She led me through a communal area where half a dozen bruised and battered faces raised themselves toward my own. My courage almost failed me then. The reasoning behind my coming here seemed threatened with obliteration by the engulfing reality of the place itself. I kept my head down, shrinking inward, as if I could make myself invisible.

We went up another flight of stairs and along a corridor.

"This is where the residents without children sleep. We call it the peace zone. The other place we call the combat zone. Just so you know what people are sayin' when you hear that!"

She opened the door onto a small room with a narrow bed and a window looking onto the backyard where I could see the children I'd heard before, playing on a swing set.

"It ain't much, but . . ."

"It's perfect," I said.

"Sister Cathy will be here later on. She's the director. Tonight's Group Night. We all have a meal together, then after . . . well, you'll see. It's special."

She showed me the bathroom I was to share with the other childless women.

"Don't be afraid to holler if there's anything else you need," she said, leaving with a kindly smile. She was fifty, perhaps; a motherly woman with an air of having made a conscious decision to ply her way through life under the flag of absolute trust and faith. I could have turned up here with a thick beard and hair billowing out of my ears and nostrils, I felt, and still been welcomed by her with the same unsuspecting warmth.

Alone, I realized I was exhausted. I lay down on the bed and closed my eyes, but at once my heart started racing and I knew I would be unable to sleep.

On a shelf by the bed were a number of pamphlets. I picked them up and looked through them. There was information on how to get a Personal Protection Order, a PPO. There was a *Domestic Abuse Handbook* with a "Violence Wheel" on it, showing eight stages in the escalation from emotional abuse to physical violence. There was a police department questionnaire: Does your partner embarrass you in front of other people? Belittle your accomplishments? Constantly contradict himself to confuse you? Use money as a way of controlling you? Hold you to keep you from leaving after an argument? Physically force you to do what you don't want to do? There was a booklet entitled *You are not Alone*, with case histories of domestic abuse survivors. Melinda was beaten unconscious when her husband found dirty dishes in the sink. Janice was kicked in the stomach after an old boyfriend came by for a visit. Meekah's arm was broken when her fiancé disagreed with her about their wedding plans.

I put the pamphlets back on the table. I felt sickened: aware, suddenly, of the scale of my trespass in coming here. My plan, which had seemed to me entirely reasonable, now struck me as a piece of insane folly. Among other things, it was dawning on me that even finding out which of the women here was the one Trumilcik had called from my office, let alone inveigling myself sufficiently into her confidence to find out anything about him, was going to involve considerably more than the few cunning, casually dropped remarks I had blithely allowed myself to imagine it would take.

I began to wonder whether this trip, far from demonstrating my ability to take the initiative against Trumilcik, wasn't after all evidence that I had fallen entirely under his control. If nothing else, that would account for the odd sense I had had since setting out, of being under duress; of submitting to a kind of strange ritual humiliation.

I sat up on the bed, looking out of the window at the kids playing in the yard, bundled up in their little faded anoraks and gloves. Two boys swung strenuously back and forth on the swings while a toddler ran from one to the other waving a plastic shovel and whimpering for a turn. A small girl slid down the slide, then ran back to the steps to climb up and slide down again. She did this again and then again, with a grim intentness; running off from the bottom of the slide back to the steps without a smile or a moment's pause to savor the pleasure of the descent. A woman in a suede coat stood watching her, puffing on a cigarette with the same intent, joyless hunger. The toddler, exasperated, hit one of the boys on the swings with his plastic shovel. The boy casually kicked him in the face, sending him sprawling in the mud, where he sat looking dazed.

I lay back down on the bed, staring at the ceiling and listening to the pipes clank in the wall until Josephine knocked on the door and led me down to dinner.

We ate at two large tables; mothers, children, and singles all mixed together. The meal was simple and wholesome, and for several minutes the conversation consisted solely of appreciative remarks addressed to the two women who'd prepared it. When one of them began trying to avert the praise, saying her pasta dish had come out too dry, Sister Cathy, the shelter director, gently reproved her:

"Chantal, do you think it really is too dry?"

The woman looked at her uncertainly a moment, then broke into a grin.

"No—you right, Sister Cathy. It's perfect and I'm proud of it. So now would you all shut up and eat!"

Everyone laughed, and the room filled with the voices of women and small children. I sat quietly, smiling and nodding, eating my food with what I hoped was a plausibly feminine grace. My neighbors were friendly without being overbearing or inquisitive; the rule seemed to be that if you wanted to talk, you would volunteer something about yourself, but not ask questions or get into exchanges beyond the response of an affirming murmur or nod.

Sister Cathy sat at the head of my table, the other end from

me. She was a broad-shouldered woman in her thirties, wearing
a flowing crimson dress. Though not immediately or conven-
tionally attractive, her appearance was of a kind that drew your
gaze powerfully in her direction. Her eyes were blue and pierc-
ing. Her dark hair shone in thick burnished waves under the
electric light. Her mouth was firm but not tight; full-lipped in a
way that suggested a developed, disciplined sensuality. I was
careful to stop myself glancing at her more often than would
have seemed natural.

After dinner Josephine led the children upstairs while the rest
of us went into the living room and sat on the sofas and chairs
with mugs of herbal tea. Sister Cathy closed the shades and
lit candles and incense sticks. I watched her circle the room,
spreading the warm yellow light from candle to candle. There
was more than a hint of fleshiness about her shoulders and
waist, but she had a dignified, almost regal carriage, and gave
the impression that it suited some queenly purpose of her own to
carry a certain superfluous bulk through the world.

As she sat down, we all linked hands and sat in silence for a
moment.

I was on a sofa next to a young woman in a seventies-style
denim coat with wide, fleece lapels. She had a choker tattoed
around her neck. She gave me an ingratiating smile and whis-
pered that her name was Trixie. In the chair on the other side of
me a large, weary-looking woman was nursing a somber little
baby. Above the hand she extended to me was a splint running
the length of her forearm. I squeezed the hand as gently as I
could.

I remember the hyperalert state I found myself in when I realized the women were going to be telling stories about themselves: I felt suddenly that I was being offered an unexpected

opportunity here, and that I needed to be especially attentive. I remember the magnetic, statuesque presence of Sister Cathy on her wooden chair, her dress hanging in crescents over her knees, her broad face golden-looking in the trembling candle flames. And I remember the women. There couldn't have been more than a dozen of them, yet in recollection the incense-filled room seems to swell and overflow, as though it had been populated by the wounded souls of half of womankind. They spoke in turn; some tearfully, some in dry-eyed detachment, some offering up only brief moments of their lives, others giving detailed accounts of entire relationships. There were poems, stories, anecdotes, abstract musings. After each woman spoke, there was an interval for discussion, comment, or in many cases merely sympathetic hugs.

Difficult as it was not to become overwhelmed by the sheer pain circulating around the room, I tried to stay focused; to reserve my attention only for things that might constitute clues relating to my particular quarry.

I caught a scent of him with the very first speaker, a thin woman with a cane, who offered a wryly told story involving an ex-husband not paying child support, a green card marriage proposal from a would-be immigrant, a financial arrangement that had "blurred at the edges," an attempt to "back away," an eruption of insanely possessive jealousy, violent assaults, and a final dramatic escape through the window of a Brooklyn apartment when the man came crashing through the door. *Trumilcik*, I had thought, picturing the maniacal figure I had glimpsed in the basement theater, bursting through this woman's apartment door. But a little later an equally plausible version of my antagonist, this time in his philanderer's guise, seemed conjured before me by a woman who read a comic doggerel ballad about a *"cheat 'n' beat"* husband whose idea of marriage was to send his wife out to work cleaning houses, while he blew her wages picking up women in clubs and bars.

> *One time the crazy bitch complains*
> *And gets her nose broke for her pains . . .*

"That's a powerful way to take possession of our anger, isn't it?" Sister Cathy said. "Turning it into laughter?"

But no sooner had I made up my mind to get into conversation with this woman after the meeting was over than another resident, frail-looking, with wide, watery blue eyes, stood up and delivered an incantation entitled "Naming the Weapons" in which, in a tremulous monotone, she catalogued the occasions of her boyfriend's outbursts of violence and the weapon used in each attack. *Morning, October,* began one of the entries, *after I telephone to my sister Jean in Poughkeepsie, the one he knows she wants me to leave him. Weapon of choice; metal bar.* And immediately I seemed to glimpse my quarry again. . . .

Too many clues. . . . The last thing I had expected! It was more bewildering than having none at all. I began to feel as though the various aspects comprising my picture of Trumilcik had been distributed piecemeal about that room. A familiar redolence of dereliction wafted up from the fitfully coherent reminiscence of a scarlet-faced woman, formerly homeless, who had been stalked by a homeless man she'd met at a mixed shelter in Rockland County. . . . Then an educated, timid-voiced Asian woman spoke of her misbegotten alliance with a man who had seemed the soul of gentleness and civility—a college professor, no less—until he lost his job, started drinking, and took to kicking and punching her of an evening, until she was hospitalized with three broken ribs and a fractured pelvis, and once again I found myself thinking, *Trumilcik.* . . .

"What about you, Marlene?" Sister Cathy asked me, as my own turn came around. "Is there something you'd like to share with us?"

I remembered my "plain-dealing" moment with Mr. Kurwen, and for an instant I imagined how similarly large-spirited it would make me feel to stand up, reveal myself for the man I was, beg their pardons for intruding on them in this way, and ask outright if any of them knew a character by the name of Bogomil Trumilcik.

But caution prevailed:

"I'm still . . . I'm still a bit overwhelmed by things," I said lamely.

"Of course."

Trixie, the girl next to me, took my hand. "Poor baby," she breathed. She shifted over and gave me an intent squeeze. She smelled of bubble gum and patchouli. It was a strange, painful delight to feel a woman's body against mine. I was careful to keep my own hands on the sofa at either side of me. After she let go, I noticed that Sister Cathy was still looking at me. Her eyes were long and narrow; set like curving willow leaves above the high, almost horizontal planes of her cheekbones. A fierce, sensual heat seemed to spill from them. As she continued staring, I realized to my horror that I was going to blush. I sat back in the sofa and lapped frantically at my tea, hoping to conceal the scarlet fire racing up over my face. But I had become luminous: I felt it; pulsatingly incandescent! My whole head was throbbing like a beacon.

The meeting ended shortly after, and I went straight to my room, too disconcerted to think of pursuing my mission any further that evening.

After a couple of minutes there was a knock at the door. I opened it to find Sister Cathy.

"May I come in?"

She shut the door behind her and stood close, eyeing me in silence. I looked back at her, not knowing what to say; feeling only that things were moving out of my control.

After a moment she spoke:

"Do you know the scientific explanation for blushing?"

I shook my head.

"It's an evolutionary anomaly. It's controlled by a part of the mind that answers to the interests of the social group rather than those of the private self. It alerts people to the fact that something duplicitous is occurring in their midst."

All her features, I noticed, were a little larger than life—her long eyes and full-lipped mouth, the high, smooth planes of her cheeks. She was like an image created to be gazed on from afar. Up this close there was something overpowering about her.

"Are you hiding something, Marlene?"

"I thought it had to do with sex—blushing," I said; an attempt to disguise my nervousness under a mask of flippancy.

A sardonic smile appeared at her lips.

"You're attracted to me?"

I shrugged. "Maybe. . . . "

Her smile remained.

"Well, I'm afraid I'm a nun," she said. "I've taken a vow of chastity."

I said nothing.

"I'm also heterosexual," she added.

"Yes."

"But perhaps that's why."

"Why I blushed?"

"No. Why you're attracted to me."

I was unsure what she meant. I said nothing. She reached her hand out to my cheek, then drew my head toward hers. Her other hand ran down across my chest, under the lapel of Barbara Hellermann's padded jacket. For a split second I thought I was about to find myself in a situation of excruciating awkwardness. But a moment later she smashed her knee into my groin and I fell to the floor, writhing.

"I know who you are," I heard her say before she left the room. "She isn't here. Now take your things and fuck off."

Chapter 11

It was Melody who had suggested the outing to the Plymouth Rock: Melody Schroeder, the actress girlfriend of Carol's colleague. Blumfeld.

I remembered this as I sat nibbling a fortune cookie in a Chinese restaurant in downtown Corinth. The place had emptied; waiters had begun stacking chairs on the tables. I had six more hours to kill before the next bus out of Corinth. I was in my own clothes now: tired but strangely content, as though I had accomplished something after all, though I wasn't sure what it was.

As I thought back to the moment when Melody had first mentioned the club, it seemed to me that I could hear her offering, as an added incentive to go, the fact that an acquaintance of hers, a colorful character, frequented the place, and that we might run into him there if we were lucky. And through the murk of elapsed time a phrase suddenly flashed out at me: *a European guy; totally bizarre . . .*

I could hear Melody saying it, clear as day. Her voice had a gravelly rasp that was pleasantly at odds with her fresh, girlish appearance, and I remembered thinking (only a little disapprovingly) that she knew this contrast was appealing.

A European guy; totally bizarre . . . The description, of course, had meant nothing to me at the time. But now, as the implications of Sister Cathy's parting remark began unraveling in me, and the circumstances of my ejection from the shelter started resonating with those of a similar confusion of identity and a similarly violent ejection after I'd made my own pilgrimage to the Plymouth Rock that night, the night of the outing, it dawned on me that her remark might not have been without significance.

Was it possible, I wondered, that in both instances I had been mistaken for the same man?

The upturned chairs were approaching like a herd of inquisitive cattle. I paid and left. Out in the damp air, I wandered through the town. Handsome old brick buildings, browed with fancy moldings, lined the streets. There were churches everywhere; resplendent edifices from the last century—white-spired wooden toy boxes, stone mini-cathedrals with florid finials and crockets. Apparently Corinth had once thrived; had had a reason for springing up here on this dreary plain, though whatever it was, there was no trace of it left. I found a bar down a side street and sat for a couple of hours, continuing to puzzle out what had happened.

After our guests had left that night, taking Carol with them to the club, I had felt piqued and a little resentful. Though I had merely tried to put Carol in mind of the healthy skepticism she would normally bear toward the kind of thing she now seemed intent on doing, she had retorted with such vehement and cutting defiance that I was left feeling as though I had been caught—I, of all people!—trying to exercise some defunct male prerogative over the comings and goings of my spouse.

Alone in the apartment, I had cleared away the dinner, trying

hard not to start reading things into Carol's uncharacteristic
behavior. We had a blissful, solid relationship: I was certain of
that. We might not have married as soon as we had if my continued residency in the U.S. had not required it, but there was no
tension attached to the fact that we did. We had had the cere-
mony at City Hall, then gone out to dinner with friends. It was
all very simple, and we hadn't tried to pretend it meant anything
more than it did. Even so, I think I was not alone in finding surprising new depths of emotion opening inside me in the days
that followed. I remember feeling undeservedly lucky in having
found someone whose every quirk and foible, from the calls she
would make to our congressman whenever an important bill
came up, to the way her fingers moved when she flossed her
teeth at night, touched off different nuances of affection in me,
as though some splendid shimmering mosaic of love were being
assembled piece by piece in my own heart.

Before this dinner party there had been no sign that Carol
felt any differently from the way I did. I told myself not to set
any store by the episode. It was a freak occurrence, I remember
thinking; a one-off, without significance. Maybe she had certain
ancient, deep-seated erotic fantasies connected with the kind of
role-playing activities Melody had alluded to. If so, she was possibly a bit embarrassed at having disclosed this, and had become
aggressive as a way of covering up her embarrassment. That was
all there was to it, I assured myself. Telling me *get the fuck off my
back, will you* in front of her friends, as she had, was just an
unconsidered outburst. It wasn't intended to imply that I had
been in any way *on* her back; that there was some prior act in
this drama which I had been unaware of playing a role in.

So, I had gone to bed. I had to be up early next morning for
my Employment Authorization interview at the INS. Carol
would be home soon, I reasoned: a few moments in this club

would be enough to remind her that the incorporeal world of private erotic fantasy was something quite separate from the lumpish, flesh-and-blood solidity of real human beings, however they conducted themselves. Her old, stabilizing scorn for the more extravagant manifestations of human folly would reassert itself, and she would be out of there.

But by two in the morning she still hadn't come home.

I was wide awake. Ancient doubts, insecurities which had seemed miraculously vanquished by the act of marriage, were creeping out of their graves. I wondered if I had once again made a catastrophic misreading of a situation; got myself entangled with another Emily Lloyd. Was I wrong about our happiness? Had I misconstrued Carol's habitual quietness as contentment when all along it was the quietness of a steadily burgeoning antagonism? The rational part of me dismissed this (after all, she had married me of her own volition), but anxiety, like arousal, has a mind of its own, and by two-thirty this mind was racing.

I felt suddenly that I didn't know my own wife: didn't know who she was, or what she was capable of doing. It occurred to me that for her to have behaved as she had, on this particular night—the eve of my big day at the Immigration and Naturalization Services, where the fundamental questions of where and how I would be able to live were to be all but settled—was perhaps not an accident. Was she deliberately trying to sabotage my life in the States; use the great impersonal levers and wheels of the INS regulations to do what she perhaps lacked the courage to do herself: separate us? Was there perhaps even an element of pure, gratuitous spite? I felt as if the ground were dissolving under me. The entire basis of my existence seemed to be suddenly in question. Somewhere in its whirling fog, my imagination conjured a scene where an immigration officer came to our apartment to check on the authenticity of our marriage, only to find no sign of an American wife at all. Would she engineer such a scene? I wondered. Could she all this time have been nurturing a hatred, conscious or unconscious, extreme enough to do such a thing?

As I'd lain there examining this conjecture, an incident from the real past had come back to me; one that I had dismissed as unimportant at the time, even if trivially disturbing, but which now seemed to contain some possibly larger significance than I had allowed myself to think.

This concerned a visit she had recently made to her parents in Palo Alto. Her fear of flying was such that she would always ask me to go with her on these rare trips. If I couldn't, she would make the journey by train. On this occasion, however, when it turned out I was unable to go, she had decided to fly alone. It was time she got over this ridiculous, irrational phobia, she had said, or at least learned to ignore it. I didn't try to dissuade her, though I felt a certain anguish: I was worried for her, but I was also a little saddened on my own account. In a strange way, her phobia had become one of the things I most cherished about our relationship. Not only did it turn our journeys together into interludes of extreme intimacy where her guard was down so completely I felt as though I had been entrusted with the care of some infinitely vulnerable child, but I had also—having made quite a study of it—come to see the phobia as a peculiar distinction.

To describe it a moment: it was chronic, extravagant in its effects, but self-contained. Carol herself seldom gave it any thought when she wasn't about to fly, and before meeting me she had considered it merely an aberration in an otherwise well-balanced disposition; inconvenient but without wider significance.

For me, though, the serial terrors she began feeling as soon as she woke up on the day of a journey by air represented a kind of spiritual badge of honor, setting her apart from the great mass of people, who dwelt—as one philosopher put it—in "the cellar of their existence." There was something otherworldly about her feelings, religious almost, like the seizures of ancient sibyls. I always encouraged her to indulge them to the full, so much so that she once playfully accused me of making a private cult out of her fear, and it was true that I was as fascinated in observing every detail of her trauma as I was intent on supporting her.

The whole journey would take on a ritualistic quality, like a sacred procession, with its own stations and advances, its own precise gradations of solemnity as we passed through the airport's successively more confined and concentrated spaces. At the check-in hall, the day's formless anxieties would converge into their first distinct manifestation: a bright, uncharacteristic chattiness, where Carol would attempt to engage every passing flight attendant in seemingly casual conversation on subjects such as the incidence of freak storms or the safety policy of their respective airlines. After that came the passage through the X-ray security checks into the more purposeful atmosphere of the departure lounge. Here, Carol's fear would begin to acquire force and discipline. Excuses to go home would invent themselves, each more flimsy than the last: she had left the stove on, the door unlocked; there was a TV program she had to watch. . . . And when I had patiently talked her out of these, she would fasten her attention on the flight information monitors, checking which flights were delayed, which canceled, divining from these dim flickerings of intelligence whole inauspicious skies. "Oh Lawrence, let's fly another day," she would implore me, and it would seem to her that nothing could be simpler or more obviously correct than to go home and try again another day. If our own flight happened to be delayed, she would gather her things and stand triumphantly, certain that with this incontrovertible

portent of disaster, she had won the right to abandon the journey; tearfully amazed when I insisted we carry on. So, with a
gathering feeling of impending catastrophe, she would follow
me down the muffled corridors to the confined, glassed-off room
reserved specifically for our flight—the boarding gate—where a
trancelike stupor of apprehension would settle on her. Warm,
melting undulations of fear would travel through her belly; her
muscles would go limp, her insides loosen. She would go five or
six times to the bathroom, feeling—she told me—as if she were
wading through a medium denser than air, hearing her heart
beat with a crunchlike thump. And then, delaying it until the last
possible moment, she would let me lead her to the low-vaulted,
thick-doored opening of the plane, pausing before it, as one
might before the charged darkness of a sacrificial chapel,
glimpsing through the divide of the curtain, the immense, green-
lit zodiac of the pilot's console; the whole vehicle humming as if
possessed by diabolic forces. And as we taxied out, and the hum
grew to a roar, and the lumbering momentum that seemed to her
at once too much to bear and yet at the same time nowhere near
enough to keep us airborne heaved us up into the clouds, the
wheels knocking and whining as they were retracted, other
noises more mysterious traveling through the fuselage—thumps
and rumbles, sudden alarming cutoffs of certain pitches—she
became wholly consumed by the terror of death. She lay back in
her seat feeling by turns a vertiginous faintness as if the life were
already evaporating from her, and a sudden, intense, unbearably
vivid alertness, as if everything death was about to take from her
had packed itself into the present moment and was bursting in
her like too much air in a balloon.

   All the while I would sit gravely by her, holding her sweaty
hands: sympathetic, curious, adoring. When we flew shudder-
ingly into a patch of turbulence, or climbed abruptly to avoid

thunderclouds, and she felt herself thrust into a still more poignant realm of dread, I would interrogate her on the precise nature of her suffering, and if she was too overwhelmed to speak, I would tell her my own theories: "What you're experiencing is a revelation of the full reality of death. . . . This is what it's like to be alive at every level of your existence. You're a house with every light blazing. . . . You're in naked contact with the actual substance of your life. You're seeing it in its full, terrifying splendor. Most of us never even glimpse it. It's a gift, like healing or clairvoyance. . . ."

It had been a surprise, then, an astonishment, really, when I called her in Palo Alto to ask how the flight had gone and she had answered me with a strange breeziness that it had all been fine, then changed the subject as if she were barely even willing to acknowledge she had ever had any difficulty flying. And on her return to New York, she had seemed almost irritated at my concern, serenely declaring once again that everything had been just fine.

That evening, as she unpacked, I had seen her stowing a small bottle at the back of her night table drawer.

"What was that?" I had asked her.

She had turned around looking surprised—evidently unaware that I had come into the room.

"That? Oh. Halcion. I took it for the flight. Dr. Elearis prescribed it for me. It seemed to work."

"Must be very powerful."

"I guess." She gave me a bright smile and returned to her unpacking. I'd stood there, feeling rather stunned.

After a moment she turned to me again.

"I thought you maybe wouldn't approve," she had said quietly. "That's why I didn't tell you."

That was all. But two weeks later, on the night of her expedition to the Plymouth Rock, as I lay in bed trying to stave off my own feelings of encroaching disaster, I found myself reliving the little pang of hurt that the incident had triggered, and this time, instead of suppressing it with a little inward shrug, I let its full resonance unfold inside me. The clandestine nature of it all—the secret visit to the doctor, the covert purchasing of the pills, the nonmention of them when she spoke from Palo Alto, the apparent attempt to conceal them on her return—all *that* I could forgive, as I knew Carol well enough to know that the motive was to spare my feelings rather than to "deceive" me in any improper sense. What stung was the act itself. That state of more-than-human vulnerability, of absolute unshieldedness from the dark terms of existence, was one of her glories, like her beautiful hair or the delicate fluting of her hands. She knew I felt this, and so for her to sabotage it, to smother it under a sedative, was an act of self-mutilation that seemed, as I reflected on it, to be aimed at me; aimed specifically and defiantly at me, its principal connoisseur and sole admirer. I pictured her swallowing the pill (minute and violet; I had looked), imagined it unfolding inside her, shedding its artificial calm in great drifting sheets that settled one by one over the disturbance inside her, swathing it in blankness. And it seemed to me that in obliterating this fear, she was also obliterating my own presence inside her, and that this, whether or not it had been her original intent, had proved an unexpected liberation.

From there (drinking this bitter cup to its dregs), I had tried to guess at her new, dread-free state of mind, and found myself imagining a kind of heightened susceptibility; a lack of resistance to other people—strange, perhaps, but doubtless rather blissful. And if that were the case, might she not have wanted to experience it again, whether or not there was a plane journey ahead? I pulled open the drawer of her night table. The pills were still there, but although I hadn't actually counted them when I had opened the bottle before, I had the distinct sense that there were now fewer of them. The thought of her drifting into Melody's club in this state of mind—tranquilized, fearless—came to me with a sudden tightening of alarm, and even though I knew that for her to do such a thing, to go out to a sex club stoned on prescription-strength tranquilizers, would be an aberration amounting to total metamorphosis, the image was peculiarly potent.

I record these things in all their doubtless rather petty detail in order to prove that I have no wish to conceal the distress I was feeling by the time I stormed out of the apartment and flagged down a taxi to take me to the Plymouth Rock on Eleventh Avenue. I was distressed, yes—hurt, even angry—but my intent was merely to ask Carol to come home, and find out what was going on—what was really going on in her heart. Violence never entered my thoughts. It never does enter my thoughts. I have a particular squeamishness on that subject. The idea of it physically sickens me. Disgusts me! The behavior I subsequently found myself accused of is so ludicrously out of character I would laugh if the episode didn't still have the power to make me weep.

The bar here in Corinth must have closed around the same time as I'd left my apartment that night in New York. I headed toward the bus station, down a mile-long avenue of small wooden homes with the winter filaments of dogwoods and magnolias spectrally afloat on their front yards. I'd drunk enough to feel numb to the cold as well as to my own exhaustion. I felt I could have gone on walking forever. The houses ended and the strip malls began: luminous gas stations and convenience stores; the great cinder-block cubes of Wal-Mart and Kmart, waiting there for the archaeologists of some postcataclysmic future to mistake them for the tombs of emperors buried with all the strange totemic objects of our time—electronic gadgets, fluffy toys—repeated endlessly like Chinese horses, pledging our unfathomable pursuits to eternity. Then the fast-food franchises—shrines of a lost religion; stupas to chicken gods and lobster gods. . . .

I came to a cocktail bar—a squat pink box with a neon palm winking in a dark window. A few cars stood on the tarmac outside, metallic night sheens giving them a look of hardened solitariness. I went in: mahogany light, almost black, with muted pink glows from little fluorescent tropical blooms.

A snub-nosed, bare-midriffed waitress with coral-pink lipstick showed me to a booth.

"My name's Terri," she said. "If you care to have a companion, I'll be happy to join you."

I hadn't taken in the other booths till then. Men in suits sat over big glasses—vases, really—of what looked like paint or antifreeze; one man per plump, sphinctered, leatherette booth; most of them with a bare-midriffed cocktail waitress like Terri perched beside them.

In retrospect I wish I had accepted Terri's offer: to have been remembered in Corinth by someone well enough disposed toward me to agree to testify to my presence there that night would have been a great help. Naturally, though, it was out of the question. I shouldn't even have been sitting on my own in such a place, though under the circumstances I think I can be forgiven for not leaving immediately.

"That's all right," I said.

Terri smiled sweetly.

"If you see someone else you like, just let me know and I'll send her over."

I mumbled my thanks, realizing the cumbersome futility of trying to explain one's code of conduct in a place like this. Like Gladstone going out at midnight to sermonize the streetwalkers of Victorian London. Bass-heavy mood music pulsed out of the shadows. There was something phantasmagorically South American about it all: wintry Corinth's fantasy of the steamy tropics. . . . What a day; what a strange day!

After Terri left I remembered my unsightly appearance again, and felt touched that nothing in her manner had alluded to it. Not like the surliness of my reception at the club on Eleventh Avenue. The man in rubber at the door there had turned away from me as I approached, not even deigning to inform me that I had been refused admittance. I paused long enough to watch a couple swanning in—a young woman leading an older man on a dog leash. Then, surging on the momentum of sheer annoyance, I backtracked to the apartment, grabbed what I needed from Carol's closet, and burned ten more dollars I could ill afford on yet another cab back to the club. Rudimentary as it was by way of a costume, the thuggish, fetus-in-a-jar effect of my stockinged head seemed to do the trick. Or maybe it was just that by three-thirty A.M. the revels within were considered too far advanced for a solitary misfit to dampen. At any rate, the amphibian at the door condescended to take my fifty dollars and let me in.

"Nothing real man, all right?"

Nothing real. . . . But the blood streaming down the appalled, familiar face I glimpsed through the fire door slamming behind me as I was hurled out not twenty minutes later had looked real enough. And the riding crop one of my burly escorts slashed me with before tossing it after me in the apparent belief that it was mine was real enough too. I knew where I had seen that: a plump man in leather trousers with the seat missing had been offering it to anyone who'd take it. I had kept well away from him, as I had—as far as was possible in those suffocatingly crowded rooms—from everyone else. *Noli me tangere.* . . . In retrospect the place itself seems of purely zoological interest. I think of

Remy de Gourmont's *Natural Philosophy of Love*, a book I have my students read for its inspired analysis of the biological underpinnings of sexual behavior. One chamber after another in the corridors off the dance floor seems like a living illustration of its pages—anthill orgies with the lovers falling in golden cascades, frogs foaming ecstatically in slime, spintrian gastropods forming hermaphroditic garlands. . . .

Was he there? I wondered as Terri brought me my beer, which turned out to be served in a fantastical tankard with a lid you had to open each time you wanted to drink. Had he seen me enter that first dark, pounding space with its mass of pulsating bodies, scanning it hopelessly for Carol at each burst of blue lightning? Had he found—bought, borrowed—a stocking to pull over *his* head to impersonate me? Could he have begun his vendetta as far back as that: before I had even been moved into his room at Arthur Clay?

And if so, why?

Why?

Chapter 12

I took the first bus out of Corinth that morning and went to sleep as soon as I got home. Late that evening I was woken by Mr. Kurwen's TVs. I went groggily into the kitchen and looked for something to eat. There were some eggs in the fridge and the stale half of a loaf in the bread bin. I remembered a dish my mother used to cook for me as a child, a rudimentary French toast she called "eggy bread," made by dipping slices of bread in beaten egg and frying them in butter. That would do, I thought; better than going out to some hip little East Village restaurant and sitting alone among the groups of young diners, trying to look like the guest of honor at an exclusive party of one.

I turned on the radio as I cooked. There was a news story about the Iraqis violating the no-fly zone. A Pentagon spokesperson said the U.S. would respond when and how it chose. "We have no intention of letting this man set our agenda for us," he declared, and I remember feeling that this was exactly the right attitude to take. After that there was a brief report about the body of a woman found in Central Park. Other than the jolt of dismay one feels automatically on hearing this kind of thing, I didn't pay it any particular attention. The eggy bread was ready, the mottled yellow and white glaze on each side just starting to brown. I put the two slices on a plate, poured a glass of water, and sat down at the kitchen table. A little joke came into my head: if Carol and I got back together in time to go to her aunt's house in Cape Cod this summer as we'd planned, I would refer to the screened porch where we ate our meals as the "no-fly zone." That would tickle her—I was sure. Just thinking of saying it, I could see her clear-skinned face light up in a laugh. She would laugh her high, austerely musical laugh, and from there on everyone—her aunt and all the other guests—would refer to the screened porch as the no-fly zone, and I would bask in the pleasure of having made a contribution to the general merriment. I found myself wishing I hadn't given Elaine the sweater I'd bought for Carol—wishing in a way that I hadn't even gone to dinner with her in the first place; that I had preserved not just the sweater but my own emotions chaste and intact for the time when Carol and I were ready to put all this nonsense behind us and start again. By the time I had thought these thoughts, overcome the inevitable backwash of self-pity that followed, and cleared away my dinner, another news bulletin had begun on the radio. This time there were more details on the body in Central Park. It was that of an Ecuadorian woman named Rosa Vasquez, who had recently moved to New York. She had been murdered sometime the previous night by a blow to the head. The reason for the attack was not known.

I turned off the radio: an irrational anxiety had come into me, and I had no wish to torment myself by purposelessly nourishing it. I read for a couple of hours, then graded papers until I was tired enough to go back to bed.

In the *Times* the next morning, there was a picture of the woman with the golden earrings. Not that you could see the earrings themselves in the blurry picture, but it was unmistakably her. The picture looked like a photo I.D., and might well, I surmised, have been a blow-up of the very picture Trumilcik had described being taken at the INS, the woman smilingly adjusting her hair to show off the earrings, only to be told to remove them by the surly photographer—*aretes!*—producing the rather glum expression on the face staring up at me now above the words *Woman beaten to death in Central Park*. The story described her as a dealer in rain forest artifacts.

I seem to have a gift for at least temporarily staving off the encroachment of bad tidings. Just as I had suspended my true reaction to the sight of Carol's Halcion that time she flew in so insouciantly from Palo Alto (only to suffer the real impact a couple of weeks later with a fierceness perhaps exaggerated by the delay), so, now, I experienced a kind of inward feinting or evasion; a sense of having been confronted with something truly appalling, and of having dodged its blow.

I spent that morning in a mood of taut neutrality. I was able to finish grading my papers; even went on to prepare my seminar for the next day. That afternoon, however, as I set off for my appointment with Dr. Schrever, I could already sense this sheeny calm beginning to discolor at its edges. Like some powerful corrosive substance, the implications of Trumilcik's latest maneuver (I could only assume it was that) had started to spread in darkly across my mind. The shape of what was being perpetrated against me had begun to clarify, though how I had managed to lay myself open to an act of such preposterously

elaborate vindictiveness, how or why such an intricate engine
of destruction could ever have docked at *my* life, was still
unfathomable.

I lay on Dr. Schrever's crimson couch in silence, unable to
think of anything but Trumilcik. I hadn't mentioned him to her
in all this time, my instinct for discretion having grown in direct
proportion to my sense of the danger he posed. Now, much as I
would have liked to unburden myself, I felt more than ever the
imprudence of adding this self-evidently deranged figure to the
portrait of my psyche that Dr. Schrever was compiling in her
notebook.

"Is there something you don't want to talk about?" she asked
after several minutes had passed in total silence. I had forgotten
the delicate humor she sometimes deployed.

I tried to think of something innocuous to fob her off with, but
my mind stayed obstinately on Trumilcik.

"You seem distracted today, Lawrence."

"Do I? I'm sorry."

"Is something the matter?"

"You mean other than my wife leaving me?" I'd meant this
to sound lightheartedly sardonic, but it came out querulous
and overemphatic. Its vehemence resonated harshly in the quiet
room.

"Are you angry with me?" Dr. Schrever asked.

"No. Why would I be angry with you?"

"Perhaps you thought I'd be able to take away the pain of your
wife leaving you. Or else help get her back. I'm assuming that's
why you came to me in the first place."

It was all I could do to stop myself scoffing out loud at this. I
felt like telling her my real reason for being there, but in my cau-
tious way, wary of alienating someone who could presumably be

counted on as an ally if I should turn out to need her support, I merely gave a noncommittal murmur.

The session limped on like this for another half hour or so, after which Dr. Schrever apparently decided to let it conclude in unbroken silence.

Lying there on her couch, I realized I had passed beyond the reach of any help she could have offered me even if I had come to her out of genuine need. She might well have had insights into my relationship with Carol, I thought, but what could she do about the disappearance of a steel rod covered with my fingerprints?

As I walked up Mulberry Street the next day, I saw a small crowd of students at the campus entrance, some of them carrying placards.

A demonstration! I felt almost cheered by the sight—so unusual in these apolitical times.

Making out the name BRUNO JACKSON, I felt even more gladdened. Word of our meeting last week had evidently got out, and I presumed this was the students making their anger at Bruno's conduct known, just in case the president should be having any doubts about following our recommendation to fire him.

Though I took no personal pleasure in Bruno's demise, I did feel that we had made the world a little safer for the students, and I had no objection to taking my share of the credit for doing this.

It was a fiercely cold morning: the banks of shoveled snow on the sidewalk had been rained on, then frozen over, and now shone like icebergs. Their lacy fringes of ice snapped underfoot with a satisfying crackle.

I heard chanting—*"No more harassment, no more abuse,"* then a rejoinder I couldn't make out, though the sentiment seemed clear enough.

There was something invincibly appealing about students, I thought: however abrasive or clumsy they could sometimes be, they had an unerring instinct for what was morally right in any given situation. With them on my side, I felt I could face any hostility from the wider world, and as I approached them, I prepared myself for a little moment of warmth. I had perhaps tended to be somewhat distant from them, preferring for obvious reasons to err in the direction of aloofness than that of intimacy. Now at least they knew how close their well-being was to my heart. In what had become a dark period for me, this approaching moment of recognition (I think I imagined they were going to applaud as I made my entrance) had a powerful effect on me. Ridiculous as it may sound, I felt almost tearful.

A silence fell as I reached the protestors. I smiled and nodded at them. Among them I saw some of the young men and women I'd traveled to New York with when Bruno took them to see Trumilcik's play. The girl with the Peruvian hat was carrying one of the placards I'd seen with Bruno's name on it. I looked at it again, and realized with a feeling of dismay that I had entirely misjudged the nature of this demonstration. FREE BRUNO JACKSON, it read. Apparently the forces of reaction, so rampant now in the world outside, had got through to these hitherto idealistic kids after all.

I tried to console myself with the knowledge that we had acted in their best interests whether they understood this or not, but the truth was I would have dearly liked their support in this dark hour.

The chant began again, fully audible now; banal, coarse, and depressingly wrong-headed in its cheap ironies:

No more harassment! No more abuse!
Give us the freedom to fuck who we choose!

An immense weariness descended over me as I moved on. I felt I could barely walk. The campus seemed to have extended its dreary footpaths an interminable length. Another image of eternity, I thought: walking forever between the Mulberry Street gates of Arthur Clay and Room 106; the parking lots, the sooty buildings, the iron-green hemlock borders, the gray clapboard dorms, distending themselves one step farther into the cold fog with every step you took. . . .

There was a key in my mailbox: small and silver. Nothing to indicate what it might be to. I thought of the words of the Pentagon spokesperson on the radio the other night: *We have no intention of letting this man set our agenda for us.* Reluctantly though, with a sense that something more sophisticated than simple defiance was required against this particular antagonist, I put the key in my pocket, making up for the minor surrender of will this represented by forbidding myself to waste time wondering what lock or door it might turn out to open.

I taught my class, ate my lunch, held my office hours, all in a more or less somnambulistic state. In the afternoon I left through a side entrance to the campus and went back to the train station, intending to go home. 1-800-WHY HURT? demanded the podiatrist's ad. 1-800-END PAIN. By then the day had warmed considerably. Winter's grip must have been breaking: it was a mild, white-skyed afternoon—the air moist, with a hint of earth in it. Barely conscious of making the decision, I crossed to the other platform and took the train away from New York.

Here were the weather-beaten old shacks again, their out-of-season lights dangling from the bleached shingles like withered blossoms. Here were the rusting truck cabins, here the abandoned fairground. Something caught my eye as this swung past: on the wooden booth where I had made out only the initials H and M the last time I'd passed, I could now read clearly the two words they stood for: HORNED MAN.

Perhaps it was just the relative brightness of this earlier hour, but it seemed to me that the words had been freshly painted. There was something irresistibly festive about the look of them; I found myself vividly imagining the jubilant crowds of some age of comparative innocence lining up with their dimes, half-credulous, half-skeptical, eager to see just how the management was going to pull off this particular piece of audacity. And by clinging to this cheerful image, I was able to ignore for some time the strange pang of hurt—as though a stranger had sneered at me—that the sight of these words had induced. *One Eight Hundred Why Hurt?* I thought. *One Eight Hundred End Pain . . .*

From the train station in its lake of gray tarmac, I walked the mile or so to Lincoln Court.

In daylight, the stillness and uninhabited feeling of the place were even more disconcerting than they had been at night. The blue mailbox on the corner had a weird, stressed air about it, as if it were willing itself to come to life so that it could scuttle away on its little legs. A parked car seemed on the point of breaking out in a cold sweat. I walked down through the long horseshoe of finished and unfinished houses: not a soul in sight. Yellowish canebrake, matted and fleshy from the winter, stood in the scrub-land beyond, then a line of trees; all of it very still, with a watchful air. I remembered a description I had read, of the way people under certain kinds of pressure perceive the physical world; its forms and textures impinging with unnatural forcefulness; spilling out over themselves. *Hypercathected,* I believe the word was. Hypercathected reality.

The house looked deeply asleep—curtains across the front windows; the garage door shut. I wondered if there was some trick by which you could tell whether or not a garage had a car in it, the way you can spin an egg to see whether or not it's been boiled. But even if the car was still there, I realized, that wouldn't prove Elaine hadn't gone away. And at the same time I was still trying to account for my sense that she *hadn't* gone away; my sense that this brother in Iowa hadn't called as Roger Freeman had reported, not that I disbelieved Roger himself; rather that this brother had been impersonated by someone else (how would Roger know the difference?), perhaps didn't even exist; that there was no car crash; that . . . That what? Beyond that thicket of doubt and counterdoubt my powers of speculation seemed unable to cast any light, petering out like a torch beam in absolute darkness.

It made me anxious, loitering by the house like this: I wondered suddenly if I was being watched, and immediately *felt* watched. Trying not to look as if I didn't want to be seen, I approached the front door and rang the bell: no answer. The door handle, which was locked, had a keyhole right in it like the handles of hotel room doors. On a reluctant intuition, I took the key that had been left in my mailbox out of my pocket. Had this been anticipated, I wondered; my coming here? But I saw at once that the key wasn't going to fit, and to the extent that one doesn't like the idea of one's apparently spontaneous decisions being somehow foreseen, this was a relief. But at the same time I realized that in some part of myself I had been considering going into the house and removing the letter I had allegedly written Elaine, and that I had perhaps all along been half-consciously hoping this key would be my means of entry; that this indeed had been my chief reason for coming here in the first place. Only now—now that I found myself obstructed in this wish—did I become fully conscious of the danger the letter up there in Elaine's bedroom posed to me.

I had given this letter almost no thought since Elaine first mentioned it that evening up in her bedroom. The revelation of its existence had been so abruptly eclipsed by the larger revelation concerning Barbara Hellermann's death, and events since then had plunged forward at such a speed, that I hadn't had a chance to puzzle out its origins, or even to remember that this was something I needed to do. Now, though, standing outside Elaine's house, I realized that without conscious reflection I had placed this letter along with the note, the key, the poster, and all the other varyingly mischievous phenomena of the past weeks, in the category of visible manifestation of Trumilcik's malice toward me. And whatever the ultimate goal of this malice may have been, I could easily imagine the importance to it of a document that appeared to form an unequivocal link between Elaine and myself.

With as casual an air as I could muster, I sauntered around to the back of the house and tried the back door lock: again without success. As I moved on, I saw that the venetian blind in one of the kitchen windows was half-open. I peered in through the angled slats, and immediately a feeling of panic exploded inside me, even though what I saw amounted merely to a confirmation of what I had already been suspecting. There on the kitchen counter was the debris of the meal Elaine and I had shared almost a week ago, still not cleared away: dirty plates and cutlery, smeared wineglasses, crumpled serviettes. Lowering my head, I could see through the narrow gaps between the metal slats to an area of the tiled floor where what looked like the remains of Elaine's quiche had come crashing violently to the ground. Small insects were crawling over the pale curds and the gray, broken, brainlike florets of cauliflower.

Any further ideas I might have had about getting into the house disappeared from me then. I turned from the window and reeled away with a sensation of being almost involuntarily driven off, the movement of my wobbly legs more a stagger than a walk. As I turned out of Lincoln Court I remembered what had seemed inconsequential at the time, that on the night of my dinner with Elaine I had left the scrap of paper with her address on it in my office. No doubt it had come out of my wallet along with the twenty-dollar bills I had left for Trumilcik. It had been in his possession. Elaine's address had been in Trumilcik's hands! He had known where I was going; known where Elaine lived. The implications of this sank heavily through me, spreading a sensation of utter horror. To the image of myself and Elaine inside her house that evening, I was now compelled to add the figure of Trumilcik peering in from the outside, steel rod in hand.

Chapter 13

The following day, as I rode the subway up to Dr. Schrever's office, I found myself thinking of her notebook. It occurred to me that, like Trumilcik's rod and the letter in Elaine's painted box, this too had become a kind of unauthorized representation of myself; at large in the world, and impersonating me in ways that could threaten to be at the very least embarrassing. I would have liked to have had it in my possession, but short of snatching it from Dr. Schrever and running out of her office with it—something I could hardly see myself doing—I didn't hold out much hope of this.

What did occur to me, though, was that I might be able to turn its existence to my advantage.

The word "alibi" seemed almost as absurd in relation to the humdrum routines of my life as "private investigator" had a week earlier, and yet it struck me that my trip to Corinth (something I had naturally had no intention of discussing with Dr. Schrever) had acquired a new significance. It was my *alibi*; at any rate as far as Rosa Vasquez was concerned. Placing myself in

Corinth on the night of her murder seemed suddenly much more important than any advantage I might gain by my discretion. And it seemed to me that Dr. Schrever's notebook was the natural choice for the document of record.

Departing, therefore, from the policy of caution that had all but silenced me on her couch earlier that week, I made up my mind to tell Dr. Schrever about Trumilcik after all. I would tell her the whole story: how I had come to suspect his presence in my office, how I had found his memoir and then gone on to discover his hiding place. I would tell her about the sheet and the rod, the vile offering he had left me in exchange for my forty dollars, the anonymous note, the Portland poster, the key. . . . I would describe (already I could feel the enormous relief of being able to do all this) my growing suspicion of his involvement in the death of Barbara Hellermann, and I would tell her how, in my attempt to track him down, I had made my strange journey to Corinth last weekend.

Without being obtrusively so, I would be very precise about the timing of my trip and return. I would give a scrupulously accurate account of the journey, describing the bus ride up there, the rest stop, the town, the shelter itself, all in the kinds of minute detail by which reality makes itself felt. I would portray the people I had encountered along the way so faithfully that even if somewhere down the line they should forget or deny they had ever met me, no one would doubt that I had met *them*. Above all, I would be mercilessly honest about my own conduct and feelings: candid to the point of incriminating myself. That way— guilty of fraud and general duplicity—I would be immune to accusations of any more serious crime.

Unfortunately, I never had a chance to implement this plan. Before I reached Dr. Schrever's office, this too had acquired a kind of protective force field; one that seemed almost physically to hoist me up and drive me back in the opposite direction as fast as I could move.

I had bought the *Daily News* as I got out of the subway, and was reading it as I walked up along the park. There had been nothing new on Rosa Vasquez in the *Times* that morning, but the *News* had a development to report, and it was as I was reading about this that I felt myself being turned around and driven back down to the Village, filled with a weird, sickened sense of the ghastly irony with which this fiasco seemed to be working itself out.

She had had a stalker, this woman. The moment I read this, the reason for her reaction to me that afternoon in the park flashed on me with painful clarity. She too had thought I was Trumilcik! What gave it all its peculiar farcical desperateness was that, after seeing me throw something into the lake, she had notified the police, who had retrieved Mr. Kurwen's glass eye from the ice floe it had landed on, so that there now existed a possible connection between the woman's assailant and this absurd, orbicular prosthesis. It was like a riddle: what do a glass eye and a motiveless killing have in common? The answer—not the true answer, but the only answer—could be triangulated, I realized, in Dr. Schrever's notebook. For all I knew, this had already been done. Hence the radical unapproachability of her office.

My apartment felt emptier and more silent than ever. I moved through it, trying to think clearly what I should do. Turn myself in to the police with a wild, still-unverifiable story about a plot to make me look like a serial murderer? Try to flush out Trumilcik from wherever he was hiding now? (But then what? Ask him politely to please stop this inconsiderate behavior?) Or go somewhere, escape, get on a train or plane till things, as they say, "quietened down"?

I was overwhelmed: stressed to the point where my mind simply froze like a stalled engine. In a vague, trancelike state, I gathered a few things together—warm clothes, passport and green card, various papers—and put them in my briefcase, not remotely knowing what I intended to do. Having done that, I immediately succumbed to a heavy, familiar inertia. I stared abstractedly out of the window without moving. So abstracted was I, in fact, that at first I thought the flickering silver light I could see out of the corner of my eye was just a reflection on the revolving ventilator fan across the courtyard. Even when I roused myself from my stupor and moved into the kitchen to throw out the few bits of fresh food I still had, it took me a moment to realize that the flickering spot had come into the kitchen with me and grown a little larger, and that this meant it had nothing to do with the ventilator fan, but was in fact an emissary from the world of pain, come to pay me another call in its familiar metallic livery.

As it grew, spreading across my field of vision like a great, sunlit shoal of mackerel, I felt a burst of childish self-pity. I found myself thinking of my mother, childishly yearning for the soothing way she had taken up the management of these migraines when I was a boy, entering so intimately into the interstices of my pain, it seemed she might be capable of assuming the burden of it herself, relieving me altogether. And then, when conventional medicine failed to help me, the way she had sought out that homeopath, the old Finn with his tiny, mysterious pills. . . . I wondered again what they were, wished I could call my mother to find out, and as the silvery obstruction vanished and the first wave of pain came crashing into my head, I felt with a pang the sadness of the state of affairs that had arisen between myself and my mother. The truth was I had lost touch with her over the years, and no longer had an address or phone number for her. I had always been aware of something not quite natural about this, but now, for the first time, I seemed to come face-to-face with its full, appalling strangeness. What was almost worse was that I had no real idea how it had come about! It was as though some deep rift or fault line existed in the terrain of my psyche, some hidden oubliette of consciousness, into which events—even momentous events like this—could fall without a sound.

The ache pounded in my head, hammering at the inside of my skull. Hearing myself cry aloud with pain, I grabbed my coat and briefcase and ran downstairs to the street. Now at least I had a specific goal to accomplish. I knew exactly where I was going: 156 Washington Avenue. I'd read the address enough times in the Manhattan directory over the past week in my attempt to clarify the mystery of an apparent connection between Trumilcik and my wife, though that particular conundrum couldn't have been further from my mind right now, fully occupied as it was by the immense discomfort of its own physical substance; that, and the fraily assuaging memory of a pair of white, cool hands pressing into my temples and forehead.

The building was an old brownstone with chipped black lions on its stoop. The name I was looking for was on a buzzer marked APT 5. I pressed it. To my surprise the door was buzzed open without any preliminaries on the entry phone. I trudged up the uncarpeted wooden stairs to the fifth floor and saw that the apartment door was open, spilling out voices and soft music. Behind it was a small entranceway with a coat stand draped in winter coats.

Almost immediately—several seconds before I became conscious of what I was looking at—I felt the same sense of being pushed away as I had felt outside Dr. Schrever's office earlier that

afternoon and at Elaine's house the day before: an invisible peri-
stalsis of space, air, light, urging me—it had begun to seem—out
of existence itself.

I was turning, still unaware of what it was I had laid eyes on,
when a voice said hello.

I turned back, and there was Melody Schroeder, a glass of red
wine in her hand. Her cheeks were pink and soft-looking. Her
hair was short, almost shaven, though the effect was also one of
softness, rather than toughness. She was looking at me with her
odd, mischievous, secretively knowing smile. A delicious smell of
cooking had wafted into the air.

"I'm Lawrence Miller," I said. "You once—"

"I know who you are."

"Well, I was wondering—"

"Yes, but I can't help you."

I paused, blinking. The slightest effort of thought seemed to
intensify the ache in my head.

"Oh, you mean—no, no, it isn't about Carol. It's—I have a . . ."
I touched my head.

Her eyes roved across my own with an aloof curiosity.

"You do, don't you?"

"That was you, wasn't it? Blumfeld?"

She smiled. Only now do I see the cruelty of that smile: the
same indolent, foreknowing expression that I note in retrospect
as I recall the moment at our table months earlier, when she had
first suggested, her husky voice all antic innocence, that expedition to the Plymouth Rock.

"Here," she said. She brought a hand to my forehead—just
one hand, the other still holding her wineglass. She was wearing
a thumb ring: gold and very thick. My eye rested on it blurrily as
she gripped the front of my head and pressed in her thumb.

There was something disturbing about it, I caught myself feeling; something delicately, elusively gross. . . .

"There. Now I'm having a dinner party which I'm afraid I can't—"

"She's here, isn't she?" I interrupted; conscious suddenly of at least a part of what it was that had caught my eye earlier: half-hidden by the other coats on the rack was the unmistakable royal blue of Carol's capelike winter coat.

"Yes, she is."

I looked over Melody's shoulder, but the corridor from this vestibule turned a corner, and the guests were not visible. From a flicker of shadow on the wall, I saw that they must be sitting in candlelight. That Carol was there, around that corner, where the voices and music and the smell of cooking were coming from, was a thought large enough to obliterate all sense of the pain in my head, and for a moment I thought Melody's touch had worked another miracle. I tried to make out Carol's voice in the drifting murmur of conversation. Just the sound of her voice would have been something to carry away with me. I could have lived on that and nothing else for days! Life itself—all I wanted of life—seemed just around that corner. A few steps and I could be a part of its candlelit, warm circle again.

"You'd better go," Melody said.

I nodded. There seemed a deep, unintended judiciousness to her words, as if she were telling me, rightly, that that unseen, golden image required precisely my own absence from it as the condition for its continued existence. As I turned to leave, I saw that the coat all but covering Carol's was also familiar, and I realized with a jolt that it was *this*—the sight of the two of them together, this black coat with its split tails joined at the stylized rectangle of raised fabric, lying over Carol's blue coat—that had created the strange force field I had felt propelling me away from here when I had first reached the doorway, and felt again now, like a great blast of cold wind ushering me back out into the night.

Bruno!

It was Bruno Jackson's coat!

He should have liv'd, Angelo says after reneging on his promise to spare Claudio's life in return for a night with Isabella. *He should have liv'd, save that his riotous youth, with dangerous sense, might in the times to come have ta'en revenge. . . .*

Like the guests on *Desert Island Disc,* I have my Shakespeare and my Bible: Barbara Hellermann's Shakespeare; Trumilcik's Bible, which, as you would expect, is no conventional Bible. Between these books I have been trying to make sense of the events of these past weeks. And it seems to me that, far from overestimating the scale and complexity of the campaign launched against me (as an obdurately skeptical part of me suspected I was, even to the end), I had been fatally underestimating these things.

That I was confronting not one, but *two* antagonists, allied against me in the implementation of a kind of vast pincer movement; motivated, on Bruno's part at least, by revenge (I have yet to understand Trumilcik's motive), was still far from clear to me as I stumbled down the stairs of Melody's building and out onto the street.

Instead of curing me, Melody's one-handed touch seemed to have made my head even worse. And added to the physical pain was that sight—an image to pierce the soul—of Bruno Jackson's coat embracing Carol's. It was about all I could do to examine the memory then of what I had had no doubt a deeply vested interest in forgetting: that Bruno and Carol had met, had spent time together under the same roof as fellows at the Getty Institute in California three years earlier. This fact had come to light last fall, when Bruno and I had first met and were sounding each other out over coffee in the Faculty dining room, cautiously trading selections of our life histories. "The Getty Institute?" I remembered saying. "My wife was there a couple of years ago. Carol Vindler."

"Carol Vindler's your wife?"

As I dragged myself through the streets of the West Village, I tried to burrow back in time to that moment. Had there been any particular glint in Bruno's eye, any suggestion in his voice or demeanor of sensitive information in his possession; of a split second's decision to withhold it? I couldn't be sure, and yet the possibility itself was enough to set my mind reeling. Bruno and my wife? *No!* I wanted to shout out the word; blast its veto indelibly onto the past, the present, and the future. Certain turns of event are simply incompatible with the continuation of one's life. . . .

I controlled myself as best I could; tried to come to a cooler, more rational appraisal of things. They had met; that was for sure. Perhaps she had found him attractive, as women seemed to. But even if she had, I doubted whether anything would have happened. The whole light-filled edifice of Carol's personality, her emotions as precise, as diamond-bright as her intelligence, was built on honesty. Deception would have been as little tolerable in there as a spitball in a Swiss watch. But now—now that she was a free agent again . . . might she not have resumed contact? Even the most contented spouses keep a few names and faces at the back of their minds for a rainy day—former lovers, someone they might have slept with if circumstances had been different, chance acquaintances their stray gaze held a second longer than a purely social contact required, leading them both somewhere they stepped back from but never forgot—and when the moment comes, the rainy day, the partner gone, how easy it is all of a sudden, how natural it feels, to pick up the phone. . . . But on reflection even *that* I couldn't quite see Carol doing. Even that had something base about it: an admission of latent duplicity during the time we were together, which her pride in her own integrity, if nothing else, would find offensive.

No, the move must have come from Bruno. He must have heard about our separation—not hard in a villagey city like New York. And he would have found a way of insinuating himself into her new orbit. Perhaps he knew Melody; knew her through . . . through Trumilcik! (That, right there, was my first intimation of the possibility of their being in league together: Bruno and Trumilcik; Bruno's cunning, his malcontent's sly machination; Trumilcik's crude and bestial brutality; Bruno pinning up that Portland poster, maybe even faking it, sticking the note in my mailbox, forging the letter to Elaine; Trumilcik crapping on my desk, attacking me in the synagogue. . . .) And through Melody had got to Carol. Ah! My insides seemed to melt. I felt as I imagined a parent would feel at the thought of their child being abducted by a stranger: an immediate, foaming panic I had to beat down, once again, to pursue the question of why he would do it. Simple opportunism? The assiduous womanizer simply obeying the law of his own instincts? Possibly. But was there not also—in the outcome, at least—something tauntingly pointed, aimed deliberately at me, calculated to send me lurching into whichever circle of hell it is that the victims of sexual jealousy suffer their torments in? Something, in other words, that might have had less to do with desire for Carol than with revenge against me? *He should have liv'd*—I read the words again—*save that his riotous youth, with dangerous sense, might in the times to come have ta'en revenge.* . . . Too bad, I find myself thinking ruefully, that the powers of the Sexual Harassment Committee didn't extend to the issuing of a death warrant!

Chapter 14

I spent that night in my office at Arthur Clay. It seemed to me I could reasonably count on a night of grace before anyone thought of looking for me there. Since my encounter with Trumilcik, I had formed the assumption that he favored the synagogue basement over this office for his nocturnal quarters, and I didn't think there was much likelihood of his appearing here tonight. But if he did, I was ready for him. At any rate, I thought I was.

I tried to go to sleep in my desk chair, but between the glare of the campus lamps outside and the unceasing ache in my head, I soon realized that this position offered little prospect of oblivion. The heat must have been lowered too, as the room was distinctly chilly. I wanted to lie down, I wanted darkness, and I wanted something to wrap myself in.

With a distinct reluctance, though realizing there was nowhere else to go (the closet was too short to lie down in), I opened Trumilcik's hiding place and crept in, closing the desks behind me.

Wrapping myself in his stinking sheet, I shut my eyes and fell into a fitful sleep, full of uneasy dreams.

I was unaware of any nocturnal visitation, human or otherwise, but when I emerged at dawn, bleary and unclean, I realized even before I caught sight of myself in one of Trumilcik's strategically placed mirrors that something truly catastrophic had come to pass.

Forcing myself to stand still and confront my reflected head, I had the sensation of fainting rapidly through successive layers of consciousness, but without the luxury of passing out.

A thick, white, hornlike protrusion had grown out of my forehead.

I knew, of course, that this could not be so; that I was either still asleep and dreaming it, or that the mounting pressure of these past few days had made me suggestible to the point of hallucination. But this knowledge didn't remotely lessen the terror I felt as I stared at my image in the mirror. Gingerly, I raised my hand to the protrusion, praying that the sense of touch—less given to hysteria, perhaps, than that of sight—would prove the monstrosity an apparition and make it vanish. Unfortunately, it had the opposite effect. The thing felt appallingly real: hard, rock-smooth, and icy cold.

Though I was no longer in pain, I felt as though I had become extremely ill. Something had shifted in my relationship to my surroundings. Physically, materially, they were unchanged, but in some essential way they seemed to be receding from me, or I from them. It was as though I had switched sides in a train, and what once rushed to meet me had started slipping away. I looked at the furnishings with an odd feeling that I recognized after a moment as *yearning*. I wasn't so much seeing these ordinary things—the black-stained chairs, the sunflower clock, the pottery mugs, the five- to seven-cup Hot Pot coffeemaker—as yearning for them. I was filled with nostalgia for them as if my world and theirs had already parted company.

All the while I was telling myself that the pale horn sticking from my forehead would be gone when I next looked in the mirror. But this did not turn out to be the case. There it still was: white and pointed, interacting with the light and shade as complicatedly as any non-apparitional body part. I assured myself that however real it seemed to me, it couldn't possibly be visible to anybody else, and that I should just act as if it were not there. Through a gap in the hemlocks outside the window, I saw a janitor wheel his mobile cleaning station into the science building across the campus, and I realized I had little time to spare if I wanted my sojourn here to pass unnoticed. But I found myself unable to leave the room. I felt that I would simply drop dead of shame the moment someone set eyes on me.

I might well have stayed there until I was discovered, had I not remembered Barbara Hellermann's maroon beret, which I had put back in the closet along with the rest of her clothes after my return from Corinth. I took it out and put it on. The horn bulged oddly underneath the baggy fabric, giving it the shape of a child's bicycle helmet—a surreally soft one—but at least it was concealed.

As I left the room I gave a last glance around, and happened to notice the book I had taken down earlier that semester—the one whose moving bookmark had formed my first, unwitting brush with Trumilcik. Impulsively, I put it in my coat pocket. Then I slipped out, hurrying down Mulberry Street to the train station.

There were mercifully few people on the train at that hour. I sat by myself in one of the reversible plastic seats, crouched down and gazing out of the window at the poisoned creek oozing along past the crumbling habitations that lined the track. I wondered what it was that so fascinated me about this spent landscape. Ugly as it was, it had something compelling about it—a strange, fallen beauty that held one's gaze in spite of one's horror. Some days, the ledges of ice shelving across the stream were pinkish in hue, some days mint green; depending, I supposed, on which gland of which deceased chemical plant or paint factory happened to have just ruptured and spilt its bilious juices into the groundwater. Even the pockets of woodland still standing here and there had a bleakly enchanted look—the trees thin and scraggly, so close together they produced not branches but parasitical-looking masses of wire-thin suckers that covered each one with a sinister furze. Bleached plastic bags fluttered up in the twigs, all one could imagine them producing by way of foliage or blossom.

It struck me that I should have brought Carol out here. With her interest in purity and pollution (when she left me she'd been writing an article on the interminable disputes over sewage and waste disposal that apparently kept the Assizes of Nuisance in medieval Europe fully occupied), she'd have made sense of this landscape. How I would have liked to be sitting by her, listening to her clear voice—always a little amused by the things her intelligence alighted on—discoursing on these matters! I found myself remembering the little colored arrows she had showered down through my father's manuscript. From there the drift of my thoughts went to my father himself—his tumor, and then the morbid question of whether I had perhaps just come into some grim physiological legacy, a notion I retreated from as fast as I could, backtracking to the sweeter image of his arrow-struck papers, whereupon I remembered a particular reference they had made; one that, in the absence of any other plan, took hold of me with the force of a directive.

However it might appear to the contrary, I had no other motive for going to the Cloisters Museum that day.

It was a cold, beautiful morning. The museum—a pantiled medieval fantasy—rose above the Hudson with a gleaming look as though it had been freshly chiseled out of the sunlight.

I had never been there before, and I was struck by how austerely the collection was mounted. There was none of the usual clutter of information and security. Stone walls and plain wooden rafters created an atmosphere of monastic simplicity. The rooms were furnished sparely, giving the eye space to study each artifact in peace. Gaunt wooden saints, gilt-emblazoned altar screens, monumental chests of drawers stood with an impassive, time-scoured look of repose. A continual chant of plainsong drifted through the rooms, and from time to time a bell tolled with an authentically cracked tone. There was even the distinct ecclesiastical odor of candle wax and oiled wood.

It was John D. Rockefeller, I read in the pamphlet I picked up, who purchased the museum's most celebrated treasure, the Unicorn Tapestries. He saw them when they were sent to New York from France for an exhibition in 1922. "I merely lingered five minutes to satisfy my eye with the beauty and richness of their color and design," he wrote, "and bought them forthwith."

The seven tapestries, depicting seven stages in the hunt of the unicorn, hang in a room specially constructed to resemble some intimate inner chamber of a medieval castle. I wandered in, the only visitor, and walked slowly around.

I was in there for probably no more than twenty minutes, but when I left the room I felt dazed; engulfed almost, as though I had just sat through some long, harrowing film full of scenes that stood in relations of dreamlike reciprocity or mysteriously revealing opposition to my own life.

Out of the stilled images of the tapestries, my mind appeared to have created a fluid continuum of action, so that I had the impression of having witnessed the entire hunt in all its vivid beauty and violence.

Right before my eyes, it seemed, the young huntsmen had set off with their spears and hounds from the flower-sprinkled glade, riding through the forest till they came upon the unicorn at a stream, kneeling down and dipping his horn to purify the waters for the other creatures of the forest. Momentarily awe-struck, the huntsmen watched in silence while he performed this sacred office. But as soon as he was finished, the spell lifted, and they closed in with raised spears and faces full of hatred. Unable to flee, the harried unicorn defended himself, turning on his attackers with a wildness that seemed out of character in such a gentle-looking creature, kicking out both rear legs at a man attempting to spear him from behind, while at the same time ripping a savage gash in the flank of an unlucky greyhound with his horn. Meanwhile a woman with narrow, beautiful, sly eyes was beckoning to the huntsmen, as if to whisper to them the secret of luring unicorns into captivity. And sure enough, the poor creature was soon at her feet, kneeling there with a look of gentle resignation, while the woman's pale hand rested on his head. A moment later he was brutally gored to death. His carcass was slung over a saddle and taken to the gates of the royal palace, where his horn was ceremoniously offered to the king and queen.

That was all, as far as the hunt itself was concerned, but in an abrupt, wondrous coda, the unicorn appeared again, miraculously restored to life, sitting in a wooden palisade against a flower-spangled background of exceptional loveliness.

Across the gallery that I came into as I left the room was a glass door to a balcony overlooking the Hudson.

I went out to get a breath of fresh air and collect my thoughts. The view over the stone balustrade was like a tinted panoramic engraving, the brightness delineating every branch, boat, and ripple with meticulous clarity. A pleasure boat appeared, NIZAM TOURS stenciled in red letters on the gray hull. The white wake behind it looked solid and immobile, lying like quartz rubble on the hammered bronze water.

I'd come out here intending to reflect on what I had just seen, but already something else was distracting me; something that appeared to be connected with what I was seeing below me at that very moment—the river, the boat, the crystalline aspect of it all.

I realize now that I was experiencing a kind of forlorn echo of my first meeting with Carol, but at the time I felt it merely as a nameless anguish, preventing me from thinking about the tapestries.

I went back inside, where I found myself in a room devoted to images of the Virgin Mary.

I didn't realize I was in a special exhibition, and certainly hadn't noticed the poster to that effect—not then, and not on any earlier occasion either.

Passing by virgins in lindenwood and worm-pocked walnut; sceptred and statuesque with baby Jesuses in their arms, or else with his rack-ribbed corpse across their laps, I came to a halt at a small triptych, an annunciation, showing the Virgin in a geometric spill of red drapery, not yet aware of Gabriel approaching in his complementary arrangement of white robes.

It was painted with a richly glowing sheen that, according to the caption, had been obtained by overlaying aqueous opaque pigments with translucent oil pigments.

As I was reading this, I felt myself suddenly rising into the air. For a moment I had no idea what was happening to me, and wondered if I truly had passed into the realm of the fantastical, a notion that grew in strength when I caught sight of the figure moving toward me from the far end of the long chamber, beyond the altarpiece, and saw that it was Carol.

An indescribable elation came into me as I beheld her; one that for a split second seemed in itself to supply abundant cause for my present levitated condition. She was here! She was coming toward me! My beautiful, radiant wife!

"Carol!" I cried.

"Get him out of here!" I heard her yell, becoming simultaneously aware of the true explanation for my airborne state, namely the presence of two large guards with their hands under my elbows, attempting to remove me from the room.

"Carol!" I called again.

"Stay away from me! I have a Personal Protection Order. You know damn well!"

"*Carol!*" I shouted, and it seemed to me I was calling across a great chasm of misunderstanding, not just separating me from her but threatening to separate all men from all women, as if we were experiencing some strange continental drift of the sexes.

"Get him away! He's not allowed within two miles of me! I already had to call the cops on him last night!"

This absurd business of a PPO! She had obtained one after being attacked that night in the Plymouth Rock.

"Listen, Carol," I cried, "that wasn't me at that club. That was—"

But the guards were dragging me away and suddenly I couldn't see her. I felt immediately a surge of power in my limbs, as though the knowledge that this might be the last chance I would ever have to explain myself released unsuspected reserves of strength. With an almighty wrenching motion, I twisted free of my captors and began to run toward Carol. As I did so, one of the guards managed to grab on to my overstuffed briefcase, causing it to fall to the ground and burst open.

I must have had a visit that night after all. Out of my briefcase clanged, of all things, Trumilcik's steel rod.

Even I, with my large capacity for expecting the enlightened view to prevail in any situation, could see that the time for explaining had passed. Snatching up my briefcase, I ran out of the room (only then did I notice the discreet exhibition poster: MEDIEVAL MARIOLATRY, with Carol's name as curator in modest print at the bottom), shoving aside the guards as they tried to stop me and racing out of the museum as fast as I could, into the desolation of Fort Tryon Park.

Chapter 15

I must have walked twenty miles, following the train line through the familiar pallid suburbs, the frayed knots of woodland, and down along the creek. The day was already darkening when I passed the podiatrist's ad. I plunged on, torn and dazed, but with a sense, at least, of being closer to the end of my journey. In a few more minutes I passed the frail shacks with their cobwebby Christmas lights, and then at last, under a cold, amethyst-colored sky, I was standing among the empty stalls and ruined machinery of the old fairground.

The door of the wooden booth with the painted sign was fastened with a large padlock. I hadn't noticed this as I sped by in the train to and from Elaine's house. Looking at it now, I felt abruptly rather foolish, as though I'd let my imagination run away with me, only to find myself brought up short by the prosaic intransigence of reality.

Leaving Fort Tryon Park, I had pictured the sudden narrowness of my options precisely in the form of this little booth. By the same token that I had clearly been expected to pay a visit to the Cloisters (why else plant the rod in my briefcase?), I sensed that my appearance here sooner or later was also expected, and I had trudged out with the distinct sense of keeping an unpleasant but finally unavoidable appointment with destiny. What had my inflamed imagination been expecting to find? Not a welcoming committee, certainly, but not the stony indifference of a locked door either. I gave the padlock a desultory tug, but it was firmly locked, and the steel hoops it was fastened through were solidly embedded in timbers that had evidently chosen to fossilize out here in the weather rather than conveniently rot. Disappointed, I turned away. Death itself might have been waiting for me on the other side of that door, and to be frank I had half-thought it was, but even so I felt cheated. The logic of necessity seemed to have evaporated abruptly from the situation: I could go anywhere at all, I realized, or nowhere. It would make no difference.

The reader of this account, not having just walked twenty miles, will surely be a few steps ahead of me here, though in my own defense I should say that it didn't take me so very many steps of my own before I too thought of what I should have thought of immediately.

It was still in my pocket. As I inserted it into the lock, I discovered, with a click that was almost as satisfying as it was galling, that in this, for once, I was right.

The place is a little larger inside than it looks from the outside. Beyond the door is a waist-high ledge, at which my predecessor presumably sat, exhibiting himself through the curtained aperture above it.

I sit here too, using the ledge as a desk, where I have been preparing a full and scrupulous account of the events that led to this enforced retirement from the world. Though the powers arrayed against me have proved themselves to be formidable, I am confident that my account will bring this unpleasant isolation to an end; perhaps even reunite me with my wife. My faith in the fundamental decency and reasonableness of my fellow women and men remains undimmed. I believe the truth will prevail, just as I believe that in a week or so the dead-looking brush and saplings outside this booth will haul up their billions of little green leaves and fragrant blossoms from the earth beneath them, however unpromising that earth may look right now.

If my enemies come—as I presume they will, having gone to such lengths to bring me here—I am ready to confront them; not in a spirit of hostility but one of forgiveness. I bear no ill will toward anyone. Having absorbed so much hatred from so many sources, I have begun to wonder whether this is not some primordial, forgotten, but perhaps still useful social function, given to me to perform, as others are given other, sweeter, more easily recognizable roles, such as leadership, say, or the spreading of laughter.

Behind the fairground is a great, smooth, curving meadow—a landfill, I suppose—with curved white plastic pipes sticking up from its surface, breathing pale fumes into the cold air. On the other side of this runs a busy highway, and a mile or so down that is a mall where I occasionally brave the stares of other shoppers to purchase candles and paraffin for the little heater I now own: my one piece of furniture. I can live easily on a few dollars a day, and at this rate I have no immediate prospect of starving.

And when I feel the need for illumination, or just for something other than my own work to distract me, I have Barbara Hellermann's Shakespeare and the book I brought with me when I left Room 106 for the last time. This latter is a translation of the Gnostic Gospels—the writings dismissed as apocryphal by the early patriarchs, and excluded from the canon of scriptures that make up the authorized version of the New Testament. Strangely enough, when I took it out of my briefcase a few days ago, it fell open on the very page I had been reading when I opened it for the first time. There before me was the passage that had so intrigued me before I was interrupted and lost my place:

If you bring forth what is within you, what you bring forth will save you. If you do not bring forth what is within you, what you do not bring forth will destroy you.

THE HORNED MAN

James Lasdun

ABOUT THE AUTHOR

James Lasdun was born in London and now lives in upstate New York. He has published three story collections, most recently *Besieged*, of which the title story was made into a film by Bernardo Bertolucci. He is also the author of three poetry collections, including *Landscape with Chainsaw*. Lasdun has taught fiction and poetry writing at Princeton University, New York University, and Columbia University. His awards include a Dylan Thomas Award for short fiction and a Guggenheim fellowship for poetry.

DISCUSSION QUESTIONS

1. *The Horned Man* is fraught with ambiguity. How does this affect the reader's approach to the story? How does Lasdun manage to spin a satisfying tale from so much uncertainty?

2. After describing his first encounters with his stepsister Emily, Lawrence Miller reflects, "Was it really possible to be so catastrophically wrong in one's reading of a situation? The discovery that it was disturbed me profoundly. I have distrusted myself ever since." How do Lawrence's interactions with Emily elucidate the story of Lawrence's relationship with his wife?

3. At what point in the novel did you begin to question Lawrence's reliability as a narrator? How is the disintegration of his credibility rendered in Lasdun's writing stylistically and structurally?

4. How does shame affect Lawrence?

5. What messages do Lawrence Miller's and Bogomil Trumilcik's stories offer about the immigrant experience in America?

6. Lawrence is the model of British formality to an absurd, self-crippling degree. What exactly is so *odd* about Lawrence?

7. Describe the clash of anonymity and individuality in *The Horned Man*.

8. How is the narrative sequence of the Unicorn Tapestries mirrored in the structure of *The Horned Man*?

9. The concept of America as a land of limitless self-invention has been explored by our greatest writers, notably F. Scott Fitzgerald in *The Great Gatsby* and Mark Twain in *Huckleberry Finn*. What new resonance does Lasdun, an immigrant to the United States, add to this familiar theme?

10. Lawrence perceives of his compatriot and colleague Bruno Jackson as a sexual predator, and is repulsed at the thought that Jackson might call on him as a cohort. How might Jackson characterize Lawrence in turn?

11. Is Bogomil Trumilcik the doppelgänger of Lawrence Miller?

12. Lawrence deceives everyone—his therapist, his neighbor, the women's shelter residents, his reader, and, ultimately, himself. Why do we still sympathize with him? Or do we?

13. Lawrence is a professor of gender studies, but women leave him at a loss. Describe the complexities of gender relations as depicted in *The Horned Man*.

14. Compare the psychological terrain of the suburbs to that of the city in *The Horned Man*.

15. How does humor factor in this deeply dark tale?

16. *The Horned Man* might be read as a portrait of sexual puritanism in contemporary America. What recent news events and popular trends does it draw upon, and why do you think Lasdun felt compelled to fictionalize this subject matter?

17. Lasdun gradually integrates a surrealist element into the novel, culminating with the growth of the horn. How does he accomplish this? Does it work for you as a reader?

Rabih Alameddine	*I, the Divine*
Brad Barkley	*Money, Love*
Andrea Barrett	*Ship Fever*
	The Voyage of the Narwhal
Rick Bass	*The Watch*
Charles Baxter	*A Relative Stranger*
	Shadow Play
Simone de Beauvoir	*The Mandarins*
	She Came to Stay
Thomas Beller	*The Sleep-Over Artist*
Melvin Jules Bukiet	*Strange Fire*
Anthony Burgess	*A Clockwork Orange*
	The Wanting Seed
Mary Clyde	*Survival Rates*
Abigail De Witt	*Lili*
Stephen Dobyns	*The Wrestler's Cruel Study*
Jack Driscoll	*Lucky Man, Lucky Woman*
Lee Durkee	*Rides of the Midway*
Leslie Epstein	*Ice Fire Water*
Leon Forrest	*Divine Days*
Paula Fox	*Desperate Characters*
	The God of Nightmares
	Poor George
	A Servant's Tale
	The Western Coast
	The Widow's Children
Linda Hogan	*Power*
Janette Turner Hospital	*Dislocations*
	Oyster
Siri Hustvedt	*The Blindfold*
Hester Kaplan	*The Edge of Marriage*
Starling Lawrence	*Legacies*

CPSIA information can be obtained at www.ICGtesting.com

229001LV00001B/78/P

9 780393 324389